T0147334

THE WOODLAND GIRLS

Quest for the Rings

Michael Miller

iUniverse, Inc.
Bloomington

The Woodland Girls
Quest for the Rings

Copyright © 2011 Michael Miller

For questions or comments please e-mail author at woodlandgirls@hotmail.com

iUniverse books may be ordered through booksellers or by contacting:

iUniverse
1663 Liberty Drive
Bloomington, IN 47403
www.iuniverse.com
1-800-Authors (1-800-288-4677)

ISBN: 978-1-4502-8934-4 (pbk)
ISBN: 978-1-4502-8935-1 (ebk)

Printed in the United States of America

iUniverse rev. date: 2/23/2011

Dedication

This book is dedicated to the most loving and giving woman I know, my grand-mother, Zona Belle Miller (1910 – 2003). This book would not have been possible without her continued support and encouragement in every aspect of my life. Her main goal in life was to serve others in whatever capacity she could. She never took credit or recognition for any of her acts of kindness. She felt it was the least she could do and was happy to do it.

You could never come to her home without being offered something to eat; some biscuits and bacon left over from breakfast, maybe some chocolate cake, or it wouldn't take but just a minute to whip up something else. At least have something to drink, she'd have sweet tea, coke, or could make some coffee. How about some milk to go with that cake?

I would like to take this opportunity to remember and thank her for being there for me and my three daughters. This story is based on the things she taught me and my girls. The number one lesson I learned from her is; what you do with a little, is what you would do with a lot.

So on behave of my grand-mother I would like to ask you to give. Give of your time, give of your money, but most important of all… give of yourself.

CHAPTER 1
THE BEGINNING

A long time ago in a land filled with wonder and magic; where ogres roam aimlessly, the Elf nation is strong, and dragons could still fly, we find our three sisters deep in the Woodland Forest. Gaea, the oldest, is twelve years old and her hair is like her father's, red as the campfire flame. It surrounds her small round face and accents her light green eyes. Naida is second; she's ten and her hair is a deep auburn and flows like water when the wind blows. She is leaner than Gaea and just about as tall. Gaea inherited their father's temper and Naida his long nose, which accented her slender face to perfection. That leaves Larissa, the youngest, who is eight and her hair is a strawberry blond. When the sun hits it just right you can get lost in a rainbow of colors. She in turn has a heart- shaped face with a small button nose and freckles, which go well with her petite form.

Their mother died in a climbing accident just a few years ago. Hardly a day goes by they don't think of her because they could see their mother in everything around the cabin. The curtains over the windows, the marks on the door post showing their height at various ages, and even the chair she sat in while she sewed their clothes by the fireside. It still hurt to think about that awful day.

Their father, Beltar, told them about how she had fallen because of a snake bite while they were climbing. He was able to grab onto a large rock before she pulled him over also but she was unable to climb with her hurt hand and he was unable to pull her up with just one hand so to keep them both from falling she cut the rope.

He searched for that snake for hours but wasn't able to find it. He kept talking about the darkness. The girls weren't exactly sure what that meant but marked it up to grief. Every since that day though, he would constantly warn them against the darkness but he still wouldn't explain what he meant.

Darkness or not, the girls having grown up in these woods knew their mother had done what she had to. That was years ago; today, Naida was worried and was discussing the absence of their father with Gaea. He had been gone for over two weeks and she couldn't shake the feeling that something was wrong.

"It's been too long," Naida said. "It only takes three days to make it to the foothills where he likes to hunt. Something's wrong, I can feel it."

"You may be right but I still think we should wait another couple days. The way game has been scarce here lately, he may've had to go a lot further than normal." Gaea replied.

Their father, Beltar, had made a habit of taking off for weeks on end since their mother died several years back, leaving Gaea to take care of her two sisters. At only 12 years old, she had to grow up fast. Of course in the Woodlands everybody grows up fast or else they quit growing at all. Gaea hated to leave Naida and Larissa alone to go and check on their dad but she was worried too. It was too close to winter for him to be gone this long without word.

"Let's give him a few more days and if we haven't heard anything by then I'll go check." Gaea stated, hoping that Naida didn't hear the concern in her voice.

"Okay," Naida surrendered. "But I still think something's wrong."

"What's wrong?" Larissa asked. She had just entered the room without the girls knowing it.

Larissa was the youngest and her sisters always tried to keep her from worrying. They hoped that she would let it drop.

"Nothing," Gaea replied. "Naida just thought that today was Tuesday."

"It is Tuesday," Larissa stated proudly.

"See, I told you, nothing's wrong." Gaea said, while changing the conversation.

"We need to stock up on firewood; it looks like it may turn cold pretty soon."

"Yeah," Naida replied quickly, as she walked out the door.

"While you do that I'm going to see if I can get something for supper. I'll be back in a couple of hours, sooner if I get lucky." Gaea said as she grabbed her bow and arrows.

She stepped out into the waning hours of sunlight in the Woodland forest. The forest was made of mostly evergreens, like pine and cedar, but there was a mixture of hardwoods scattered throughout. She decided to head toward the lake. There were quite a few oaks in that area Rule # 47, stay away from oak trees when traveling, the acorns under foot can sound like thunder in a quiet forest. Even though there's a risk it's still the best place to grab a few squirrels for supper. Rule #47, her father had a hundred or more and they were all Rule #47. Don't stare into the fire at night or you'll be unable to see into the night. Always keep up with your flint and works for starting a fire, you never know when it might come in handy. Always Rule #47. He was constantly teaching them more and more. Every time he would go into the woods, he'd try to teach them a new plant to use, a better way to travel without leaving signs, or another rule about something or other.

Yesterday she had seen sign of an ogre down by the lake and wanted to see if there was anything new. This way she could check the area without worrying her sisters and maybe get something for supper at the same time. Why were the ogres so restless lately? It didn't make sense for one to travel this far south.

Ogres were mean and ruthless, and loved to eat the flesh of anything, especially humans. They grew to about nine feet and were a three-fold creature, which meant they lived about three lifetimes of man. One good thing about them, they didn't like each other either. They're tough enough to kill but it would be worse if there was more than one.

There's just no way would she leave her sisters alone right now, not for that long. If she had to go and search for their father she'd have to take them along. That wouldn't be too bad because Larissa could easily keep up and Naida was good with a bow and knew more about plants than she did. It's just that she was worried about leaving the place with the ogre so close by. Why did their dad always do this to her? He left and all the decisions and responsibility fell on her shoulders. She decided they would leave first thing in the morning. If nothing was wrong, then good. If something was wrong then the sooner they left, the better.

Meanwhile back at the cabin, Naida was chopping wood. It was the perfect pastime for her to think, let her mind wander, and dwell on whatever was bothering her while her body went through the motions of work. She just knew something was wrong; she had the same feeling as she did when their mother died. Their father was never the same after that, he would be gone for weeks on end but this time was different. Something was wrong and she had to convince Gaea when she came back.

She had a large stack of firewood by the time Gaea returned with two squirrels and a rabbit for supper and was glad to hear they were in agreement on going in search of their father. They talked of their plans while they prepared supper. Now, how to tell Larissa?

"What do you think about a little trip, Larissa? Gaea asked while they were eating.

"Great, I love traveling. Where are we going?" she returned.

"I thought we might go find dad in the foothills and see if he needed any help. It might be our last chance to get out before winter." Gaea answered.

"Wonderful, I'll go pack right now." Larissa said, barely finishing her food before climbing the ladder to her room.

"That went well," Naida said. "She doesn't seem to be worried at all."

I know what's going on, Larissa thought while she was packing. *They must think I'm stupid or something. I can tell they're worried about dad, but I hate the fact that they won't come out and tell me the truth.* She was used to them "trying to protect her," but it was starting to get old.

Early the next morning the girls set out on their journey. It usually took three days but they were going to try and make it in two. They headed west.

Gaea explained to Larissa, "To get to the Shaderack Mountains, you had to put the morning star to your back and head toward the setting sun."

"But the sun doesn't set while the morning star is in the sky." Larissa stated proudly.

She knew that you started with the morning star and ended with the setting sun, but she liked aggravating Gaea. Maybe just a little too much.

"You know what it means," Gaea replied. "Don't be so… obstinate or I'll quit trying to teach you anything."

"Don't call me names," Larissa countered.

Naida returned from her scouting expedition just in time to see Gaea roll her eyes toward the sky and mutter something under her breath. She was worried about the signs she had seen and needed to talk to Gaea alone.

"There's a shortcut up ahead that I think we should take." Naida said, while giving Gaea a secret look.

"There ain't a shortcut ahead," Larissa said. She'd had enough of this secrecy. "I know what's going on. I can see the sign as good as you can, so would you please quit trying to baby me."

"You may be able to read sign but you need help with your English." Naida said.

"How long have you known?" Gaea asked, slightly amazed.

"We first crossed the tracks down by the lake. Why? How long have you known?" Larissa asked.

"Alright, that's enough you two," Naida jumped in. "We have enough trouble without you two starting up. Did you also happen to notice that it's the same one?"

"You mean," Larissa asked slowly, "it's the same ogre? But why?"

"He's tracking us and we need to be very careful," Naida said hurriedly. "Ogres are made for traveling in the woods with their long legs and he's been walking circles around us. He may be waiting anywhere up ahead."

It was getting late so the girls decided to make camp for the night. They kept a watch but neither of them slept very well. They were up before dawn and on their way quickly; eating only some trail jerky.

They followed the path until it came to a clearing. They worried about crossing in the open but it was too far to try and go around. They separated so that they wouldn't all get caught in a possible trap and the other two could come to the rescue. Gaea went first and her sisters followed about 50 yards back, so she was the first to see him. The ogre was looming large on the other side of the clearing just at the tree line.

It was the first time she had ever seen one. She motioned for them to stay low and catch up. They had to decide what to do.

"Wow," Naida exclaimed. "He's huge."

"And ugly," Larissa finished.

"Shh," Gaea whispered. "Do you see those big ears? He could hear you. Do we go around or fight?"

"Well, he's trailing us so even if we get away now, he'll keep coming and next time we may not be so lucky. I say we fight." Naida said.

"I agree." Larissa chimed.

"Ok," Gaea said, "from what I understand ogres are slow and…"

"They ain't slow," Larissa interrupted. "He was able to keep up with us… wasn't he?"

"Not that kind of slow," Gaea continued. "His thinking is slow. His mind is kind of one track, it takes him time to react so we should be able to out maneuver him."

"But he's extremely strong," Naida added. "If he hits you with that club of his, it'll knock your head off. So be careful."

"I think we should go straight at him," Gaea suggested. "Since we can't sneak up on him, we'll walk slowly so we can study his reaction and on my signal we fight."

The girls were in agreement, which didn't happen often. As they approached, the ogre just stood there waiting and watching. The girls stopped when they were close enough to see the red in his eyes. The ogre then started walking slowly forward and as he closed the distance the girls separated and surrounded him. Gaea had an arrow notched; Naida with spear in hand; Larissa was ready with her knife when all of a sudden it happened.

"YOU……HARD……TO………FIND…" the ogre spoke.

He travailed over each word, like a woman giving birth, before releasing it into the air to linger like the stench of his breath. The sound reverberating in their ears until the next one boomed into existence.

"…GAR…" he labored, while pounding his chest.

The girls were frozen with shock. Never in their wildest imagination had they ever thought an ogre could talk. Actually, they had not given it any thought at all. This changed everything because he had sought them out. He had purpose. He was able to think and do and live. It went against everything they'd ever heard about ogre. He wasn't just a mindless creature anymore. He was… He is…… Gar, but what did he want? Why was he looking for them? The girls had more questions than they could express.

"COME……WITH……ME…" the ogre continued.

"No," Gaea replied.

Could he really understand or was she just wasting her time trying to explain? She would love to find out what this was all about, to get some answers to the thousand questions she had, but it had to wait.

"We have to check on our father," she continued. "We have to go to the Shaderack Mountains near Chesapeake Falls."

She stood ready, weapon in hand, waiting to see what his reaction would be. She glanced at her sisters and knew she could count on them if things went wrong. It seemed like an eternity before he shrugged and nodded, then turned and led the way. It was all the girls could do to keep up. It was close to dark when they called to him to stop. Ogre could see very well at night but they couldn't. Also it was at least another three hours to reach the waterfall and they didn't want to arrive at night.

They set up a cold camp (no fire) but it was still warm enough at night and they had dried trail meat to eat before turning in. The ogre blended into the woods and returned shortly gnawing on a rabbit. The girls decided who would take the watch and the others fell into a restless sleep. It had been a most unusual day and they had no idea what tomorrow would reveal.

First light found them well on their way and after a few hours they started noticing an unmistakable smell, dragon-fire. They found the camp, at least what was left of it. The tent was a shambles, the fire-pit was destroyed, and the supplies were scattered all over the place. The smell of roasted flesh was distinct especially mixed with the smell of dragon-fire. Fearing the worst, the girls searched through the destruction. During the search, the girls recognized items they knew belonged to their father, like the old coffee pot, or the pit stake that he had carved out of stone wood and last of all Gaea found his sword. He would never go anywhere without it. They finally found the body but it was unrecognizable; still it had to be their father.

As that thought began to sink in, Naida began to survey the scene trying to determine just what had happened. Evidently, this all took place just after he arrived here two weeks ago. From the smell of dragon-fire it went without saying that a dragon had attacked, but why? Despite all the lore, dragons don't eat human flesh and the remains seem to prove that. So why did it attack?

The ogre had remained back in the woods and started making his way over to the girls as they discussed what had taken place.

"The dragon landed over here close to where I found the sword and it looks like his tail is what knocked the tent over." Gaea began.

"Yeah," Naida continued, "and there is blood here that definitely belongs to a dragon because of its green tint."

"……TWO……" the ogre spoke from behind.

"Two? You mean two dragons?" Larissa asked.

That made sense their father would be able to fight off one dragon, or at least escape without much harm, but two? She saw the ogre nod and then sniff the air. Dragon-fire has its own unique smell and is as different from one dragon to the next. Just like no two people are the same, the scent of dragon-fire varies from dragon to dragon. The ogre was right, now that she was looking for it, she could tell the difference between the two smells. The girls looked at each other as they let that sink in. The more they discovered, the more questions they had.

"……DARKNESS……" Gar spoke and the sound chilled the girls to the bone.

Their father was dead and now, Gar talks of darkness. What did it all mean? Where was this darkness? It just didn't seem real, Gaea imagined her dad the way he was when he left just a few weeks ago. He was too young…too… strong… to be…dead. What was she going to do now? Their grandmother lived in the village of Truitt, on the eastern edge of the Woodlands. Maybe they could go there. She had never seen her grandmother but her dad talked about her all the time. He had even promised to take them one day. Now he never would. The thought of how angry she had been at him weighed heavily on her mind. Forgetting about the ogre, she turned to her sisters. "We need to go to the village of Truitt." Gaea stated flatly.

"……YES……" the ogre startled them with his reply. "…… ZONA……"

The girls were stunned; Zona was their grandmother. Did she send the ogre? Did it have anything to do with all this? How could she have known?

They had so many questions and no answers. Finally they all agreed to go. Now to the business at hand, they took turns digging the grave. They made a marker out of two crossed limbs. Naida carved just one word on it, in big bold letters---BELTAR. The sisters were quiet while Gaea said a few words over the grave, then they began gathering what they could from his belongings. The emptiness was over-whelming, now both father and mother were dead. They felt all alone in the world, but maybe the grandmother they didn't know could at least give them some answers. The sooner the better.

They stayed up that night, lost in their own thoughts, and while the girls were reminiscing and telling stories about their father, they heard the most wonderful sound drifting on the breeze. They followed it to the top of the hill where they found Gar, arms raised, singing to the stars. It was more like humming, with clicks and clucks mixed in to make a three part harmony like nothing they'd ever heard.

"Notice he's not moving his lips," Gaea said. "That's why it flows so free and easy."

"You're right," Naida agreed. "It must be forming the words with his lips that cause him so much trouble when speaking."

Larissa said what they all felt. "That sounds so beautiful."

".......BELTAR..."

They understood. He was singing for their father, after all the things they thought and said, he still paid such a tribute to a man he didn't know, or did he? How could they have been so wrong about ogre? Was this what they all were like or was he special? Maybe this too could be answered in Truitt.

The girls stopped by their cabin to gather their things on the way to the village.

They were amazed with the things that Gar could do. He furnished most of the meals on their journey. He hunted with a rock. He could sling it so hard and accurate that he usually killed what he aimed at. It seemed that even though ogres couldn't think fast, single thought with them was so concentrated they rarely missed, even fishing. He could reach into the water and grab a fish almost every time.

By the time they arrived in Truitt, the girls and Gar were the best of friends. They made quite a stir when they walked through the village but they weren't sure if it was them or Gar. He led them straight to the house of Zona. It was a blue two-story, the largest cabin in the village not counting the Inn down the path. The girls were a bit nervous as they knocked on the door.

"Hello," Gaea called. "Is anybody home?"

"Yes, yes, come in." Zona replied. "Come in and have a seat. You must be my grand-daughters. Are you hungry? Can I get you anything? What can I do for you?"

"We'd love some answers, please." Naida replied. "We have so many questions and we hope you can answer them for us."

They found out she had sensed there was some kind of trouble with Beltar. This happens sometimes concerning loved ones. She'd sent Gar, as soon as it happened to find out what was going on and hopefully to bring the girls here to Truitt. The girls also learned that ogres were peaceable creatures and had many villages north of the Woodland Forrest. It was only the renegades that were expelled from the villages that caused such destruction and havoc.

The girls and Zona sat around her table and talked for hours. They broke down crying as they told what had happened at the campsite.

"There is a great darkness moving across this land," Zona began, drying the tears from her eyes. "Your father thought he could protect you and your mother from it by moving into the Woodlands."

"Our father talked about this darkness when our mother died but would never explain what he meant." Gaea said. "Do you believe that this darkness is what killed our father?"

"Yes, yes I do," Zona replied. "It has been growing in strength over the years and spreading its tentacles further and further in seemingly unrelated acts of destruction."

"Do you know what it is?" Naida asked.

"Only that it is a great evil that is spreading across the land." Zona replied. "It has been growing in strength for years and one day there will be a great battle."

The girls were especially interested to learn that Zona was a Ring Master. She possesses the ten Rings of Power: Choice, Truth, Hope, Knowledge, Honesty, Love, Responsibility, Patience, Friendship, and Happiness. These rings help her in every day life, because there are certain lessons you must learn to be able to earn the rings. The rings help to keep these lessons in your mind by heating up when you violate them, so hopefully you won't make the same mistakes again. For instance, if you had the Ring of Truth and told a little white lie it might tingle a little but if you told a big lie it would probably blister your finger. That is why Ring Masters were so valued as mediators and judges.

"We can't believe that we were so wrong about ogres," Gaea said. "We have always heard about how mean and terrible they were and now to find out how good they can be takes some getting used to."

"Yeah," Naida agreed. "And they have so many surprises too, like being able to sing so beautifully."

"Don't forget about being such good hunters too." Larissa added.

"It seems you've learned some valuable lessons then," Zona pointed out, "like not to jump to conclusions before you have all the facts."

"It's like the old saying," Larissa continued. "You can't judge a book by its cover."

"That's exactly right!" Zona finished.

"Do you think you could teach us how to earn the Rings of Power?" Gaea asked

"Sure if you study hard and mind what I say," Zona replied. "I'd love to teach you. There is a great need for Ring Masters. But either way, you are more than welcome to live here."

The girls agreed, and as they were headed up stairs to go to bed, Gaea thought about how good it would be. Through all the tragedy and hardships it seemed that fate had brought them here. Now she could be a kid again…they all could. Soon they would be on their way to earning the Rings of Power… Then the darkness had better watch out.

CHAPTER 2
CHOICE

Spring-time found the girls settled into the village life and loving it. Zona was teaching them many things about the surrounding area like plants, herbs and trees that they didn't know about the forest. Zona feels the girls are finally ready to try for the first of the rings, the Power of Choice.

The Power of Choice is the first one because all the other rings hinge on their ability to make the right choices. Zona is explaining again the test they must fulfill, in order to achieve the ring.

"All you have to do is bring back a leaf from the tree in the midst of the swamp. The ancient oak tree is centuries old, and its leaves are able to heal," Zona says. "But remember, you can only bring one. Anymore than that and terrible things will happen."

"What kind of things?" Gaea asked.

"You really don't want to find out." Zona answered.

"How will we know if we've got the right tree" Naida asked.

"The tree is lit by magic, visible both day and night," Zona answered. "The start of the path you need is north of the village, just past the large rock. The path leads through the swamp and it's a dangerous place, so once you are on the path, do not stray from it. Remember your teachings and you'll be fine. One other thing, do not return the same way that you go. There are several paths that will lead you back. Choose wisely."

The girls felt confident that this would be a breeze. If all the rings were this easy, they would be masters in no time. Gaea was the oldest, so she would go first. They had to go separately because earning the power of the rings is an individual responsibility, it can't be shared.

Gaea was anxious so she left early the next morning, without eating breakfast. This was going to be so easy. She arrived at the big rock just after sunrise, and started down the path. It was still a bit dark under the trees, but Gaea figured it would brighten up soon enough.

She hadn't gone far, when she came around a curve and there it was, bright as day. It was just across the valley but the path didn't go that way. This had to be a test: *Are you smart enough to take the shortest route, or will you go the long way around?* Gaea figured that getting to the tree was the important thing, not how you got there, so off she went. Heading down into the valley, she thought, man this is going to be so easy.

Things were going good, until she reach the bottom of the hill, that's when it all came crashing down on her head. Literally, a limb broke and fell right where she was. If she hadn't been so fast it would have hit her on the head. Unfortunately, when she jumped, she landed in quicksand. She could hear Zona now, "Out of the frying pan and into the fire."

There was a vine, knocked down by the limb that fell, if she could just reach it. It was too far away, but she was able to reach a stick close by. Using the stick she pulled the vine close enough to grab and slowly began pulling herself out. Unfortunately, the vine pulled loose before she was able to get out. She saw movement out of the corner of her eye which turned out to be an alligator. She made a noose out of the vine and was able to lasso the gator as it moved away; it easily pulled her out of the quicksand.

She was so tired and worn out from the ordeal she had to rest for hours, so much for her shortcut. She was finally able to start up the other side, but it turned out to be steeper than it looked. After several hours, she was only half way up, and had to stop to rest again. She was wishing she had brought something to eat now. If it wasn't so far back, she'd go and get that gator for lunch. Well, another hour and she should make it to the top.

Finally, after what turned out to be another two hours, there was the tree. It was huge and all the leaves were out of reach, at least from the ground. She could try and climb it, but it was so big around that would be difficult. What about throwing a stick up and knocking some leaves down? She was supposed to bring only one leaf back, and she wasn't sure what she could do with the others, if she knocked more than one down. The leaves were too valuable to waste, so she decided to climb. As she approached the tree, a limb lowered and she was able to pick a leaf without any trouble at all.

As she prepared to leave, she wondered, *since I didn't come the path can I go back that way? No, I think not.* At least, she wasn't going to take that chance. She picked the first return path she came to because it looked to be the shortest and she was very tired and all she wanted was to get home.

She arrived home shortly before dark with her leaf and gave it to Zona. She was told not to speak of her trip, until her sisters had finished. So she ate supper and went to bed. It had been a long, hard day and she could hardly wait to get into bed.

Early the next morning Naida was ready to go. Zona saw her off after breakfast and went over the instructions briefly, one more time. Take the path at the big rock, stay on the path, only one leaf, and return a different way, no problem she had this.

Naida arrived at the rock north of Truitt before sunrise, while it was still dark. She sat down to wait for the sun to come up, since it would be easier to see with daylight in the woods. She was thinking about this quest while she waited. Gaea had returned late yesterday and Naida was hoping to beat her time on this quest. It was nothing personal, just a sister thing. That's why she left so early this morning, to get a good head start on Gaea's time.

Naida started into the woods at first light, it was a little hard to see but the path was good so she didn't have any trouble. As she rounded a curve, she could see the tree across the valley and she saw where Gaea went down the hill. If Gaea could do it, so could she. Naida headed downhill at a pretty good pace. As she reached the bottom, she saw the quicksand, and was just barely able to miss it. *Boy, was that close!* She'd have to be a bit more careful in the future. Naida saw where Gaea had gotten out and started up the other side. She could tell several places where she had slid back down on the rocks and slippery sides. She decided to go back up to the path.

By the time she made it back to the path, it had taken several hours and the sun was well up in the sky. She could have kicked herself for wasting so much time, and decided to double-time it to make up for the lost time. No wonder it had taken Gaea so long. Well she was on her way now and making good time. After another two hours, she stopped for a break. Good thing she had brought a snack

Feeling refreshed, she set out again. Naida noticed how beautiful the woods are, and decided to slow down for a while and enjoy the walk. She noticed a mother deer and her fawn, they were getting a drink down by the stream, and the two chipmunks were playing around and around on a maple tree. Then she noticed a plant Zona had taught them about, called Monk's head or Friar's cap, because of the shape of its flowers. It was also known as Wolf's bane. The color varies between blue and dark purple or sometimes yellow. It grows in the woodlands and meadows and stands about 4 to 5 feet high. It's a perennial so it's present all year round even though the flower is seasonal. This plant is extremely poisonous and must be handled correctly or the user may wind up the victim.

She couldn't pass up an opportunity to gather a find such as this. There were so many possibilities to use such a plant. The juice of young tubers can be used on the tips of arrows and spears to make them more effective. In a diluted form it can be used as an external pain reliever by an expert because it is absorbed through the skin. If you happen to swallow it you can drink large amounts of water soon after and the chances of survival are pretty good. She was thinking on these lessons when she noticed the old Oak tree; she was there already.

The tree was huge; she stopped for a moment, wondering how to get the leaf. She saw a stick lying by the path and picked it up. She figured she could knock one down with it so she let it fly, and it got stuck in the tree. *At least, she thought it got stuck.* The tree caught the stick and threw it back at her…hard too. It would have taken her head off, if she hadn't ducked just in time. So much for that idea, she decided to try and climb. As she got close to the tree, it took a swing at her. Again she ducked.

"Okay, okay, I surrender," Naida said. "I wasn't trying to hurt you; I just need to get a leaf. That's all, its part of my test for the rings."

As she finished speaking, a limb lowered itself nice and slow to within her reach. Naida picked a leaf and said thank you, and was on her way in no time. She still wanted to beat Gaea's time so she picked the first path home also. Naida was thinking as she walked this was the first time she had ever been attacked by a tree, and hoped it was the last.

Since coming to Truitt, she has learned a lot about different beings, like ogre, elves and I guess now trees. It was this thinking that kept her company on the return trip. Life certainly had many twists and turns, but that just kept it interesting. It was mid afternoon when she arrived at Zona's and gave her the leaf. She too was instructed not to speak of her trip just yet.

Larissa awoke the next morning, anxious to get started. She ate a good breakfast and fixed a sack lunch to take with her. Never hurts to be prepared. Zona went back over the instructions with her again. Take the path at the big rock, stay on the path, take only one leaf, and return on a different path. Larissa said good-bye and started on her way.

It was past sunrise when she arrived at the rock and she had no trouble at all seeing in the woods, so she continued on her way. After a little while, she came to the place where her sisters had gone off the path. As she was wondering why they left the path, she noticed the tree in the distance. It did look like it was shorter but Zona said to stay on the path, so she continued on her way. Eventually, she arrived at the tree and was amazed at how big it was. How was anybody supposed to get a leaf off a tree that big?

She decided to think about it while she ate her lunch. Yeah, it was a bit early for lunch, but it was never too soon to eat. While she was eating, she noticed two squirrels playing near by. As she watched them it was as if she could tell what they were thinking. One would run and the other chased it around and around the tree. She could just imagine their thoughts; *catch me if you can.* After eating, she made her way to the tree to see if see could climb it. As she approached, the tree lowered a limb so she could pick a leaf. Boy, this really was easy. She picked the second return path because it seemed to be the largest and best. The return trip was uneventful and would have been boring if it wasn't for the beautiful view. She loved being in the woods, seeing all the animals playing, hearing the birds chirping, and the flowers blooming, it was a wonderful time to be alive.

Larissa arrived back at Zona's just as the others were sitting down to a late lunch. She gave her leaf to Zona and sat down to eat. After eating, Zona and the girls cleaned up and then sat back down at the table to talk.

"Well," Zona started, "you each have brought back a leaf, so you've earned your first ring. Did you happen to learn anything along the way?"

"I did," Gaea replied. "I learned that when it comes to making choices, convenience or how easy it seems shouldn't be the deciding factor. Something may look shorter or easier, but if it's not right, you shouldn't do it. When it comes to doing right- don't take shortcuts!"

"I learned something too," Naida continued. "You should not make your decisions based on what someone else has done. Just because someone else did something, that doesn't make it right. You should do what is right, no matter what others do or think."

"Oh one other thing too," Naida added quickly. "DON'T THROW STICKS AT TREES!"

"Very good," Zona replied, beaming proudly, "Larissa what about you? Do you have anything to add?"

"I sure do. I learned that if you'll do the right thing, it usually turns out easier. I don't believe I've ever heard of anyone getting in trouble, for doing what's right." Larissa finished.

"I am very proud of all of you. You not only earned your first ring, but have learned some very valuable lessons, too." Zona said.

The next full moon, there was a big celebration planned. Everybody would be there; even the elves were going to come. Elves are a ten-fold creature; that means they live about ten of our lifetimes, so they don't usually get involved with human ceremonies. They were coming mainly because of their respect for Zona, but they were anxious to meet the girls, since they were striving for the rings. This excited the girls even more than getting the ring. They would finally get to meet the elves, even Prince Chanook of Glendale was coming. Glendale was the Elf Nation and it bordered Truitt to the south.

The day of the celebration finally came, and the girls were excited. They even had new clothes for the ceremony. The elves have been arriving all day and people were coming from as far away as the Shaderack Mountains. Even Gar was there. Gar was the ogre that had led them to Zona after their father died. That thought saddened them a little, they wished he could be here to see it, but life went on.

The girls made their way to the center of the village, where Zona was waiting. She called the girls one at a time, onto the stage that was built for this occasion. As she presented the rings, the crowd cheered and whistled. It was so exciting, and even a little embarrassing. The girls weren't used to this kind of attention.

Then the feast began. The girls got to sit at the table with Zona, Prince Chanook, and the chief of their village, Goridon. After eating there was music and singing. It was a night they wouldn't soon forget. Zona and the girls talked on the way home.

"Well, what did you think about that?" Zona asked. "And what was your favorite part?"

Gaea said, "It was GREAT. My favorite part was on the stage getting my ring. Everybody was looking, even Prince Chanook. He's kinda cute especially his little beard."

"Yeah, and two hundred years old," Naida replied. "My favorite part was the music and singing."

"That was all okay," Larissa said, "but my favorite part was the feast. Everything was delicious and there were some foods I'd never had before. I love new foods."

"You love any food." her sisters said together.

"Oh yeah? I'll bet you I can beat you to the house." Larissa yelled as she started to run.

"That's not fair," Gaea yelled after her. "Just wait until I catch up."

Naida stayed back with Zona, as the other two raced off toward the house. It had been a long day and Naida enjoyed this time, alone with her grandmother. Things were really looking up for them here. They were a part of something worth while. She was looking forward to their next ring but something was bothering her.

"You're not going to leave us too, are you?" Naida asked

"No, my dear," Zona replied with a smile. "I'm not going anywhere, at least, not until Larissa can fix her own hair."

CHAPTER 3
TRUTH

As the story of the Woodland girls continues, we find the girls have had some success using their ring. They'd discovered that having the power of choice didn't mean that they would always make the right choice, just that they had the ability to make the right choice. As it turns out, it's one of these choices that led the girls to their second ring…The Ring of Truth.

The girls Gaea, Naida, and Larissa, were starting to get used to the life of the village. They were well known, mainly from the ring ceremony, but also from their antics. They were used to having to do everything themselves, and sometimes it gets hard to consider others, like the time Gaea was hunting.

Gaea had taken her bow and went into the woods to hunt; this wasn't anything new. She would just walk along until she cut some sign, and then she would stalk the deer, or whatever, until she found it, then shoot it, dress it, and bring in back home. Well, this day there were other hunters in the woods and they didn't appreciate her "trampling around in the woods". They claimed it scared all the game away and that was why they came in empty-handed.

Gaea apologized to them and tried to explain, but they were having none of it. She decided they were ready to go in anyway, so she continued hunting. It wasn't long until she found a deer trail, which she followed to a clearing. There in the middle was a nice size buck, she slowly raised her bow, with arrow notched, and let it fly. It went true to its mark and she had plenty of meat for the village.

That was how village life was different from what they were used to doing. Normally if you made a good kill, you would eat what you could and then put up the rest (by salting it or drying it out for jerky). Now, the food you bring in goes to the village, which was good. It splits the work load that way, some farm, some split wood, some hunt, some sew, etc…

The other hunters would get mad sometimes when the girls would bring food back and they didn't. The same went for weapons training. The men of the village couldn't understand how or why the girls were so good with their weapons. They didn't realize that the girls had to live by their weapons for years on their own, until just here lately. Gaea had been training with her father's sword and was starting to be able to best, most of the men in the village. Her teacher, Hans, said that she was a natural. She loved swordplay, it was like a dance, she would say. You parley, feint, then jab, she felt it was like a very graceful dance.

Needless to say, the girls were loved by the village but at times tolerance was needed concerning the girls. Like the time Naida's stink bomb went off in the village. Naida had learned how to mix sulfur and water together to make a horrific odor causing concoction. It was great for discouraging an animal that wanted to get too close or a practical joke on your sisters. The villagers had to avoid that area of the village for a few days.

It was another of these situations that led the girls to the next ring. Gaea had over heard some elves talking one night after the ring ceremony. It seems the elves were going to celebrate their new year at the next full moon. Elves are tall, slender creatures, similar to men but live a lot longer. They had pointed ears, fair complexion, their hair was sandy blonde and their skin was tinted a light green. This enabled them to hide very well in the woods. An elf couldn't be found if it didn't want to be, and this was an Elfin Ceremony, and humans were not invited.

Gaea had been thinking on this for about three weeks and had finally come up with a plan. It was another week before the New Year and she was going to need some help to pull this off. First, she had to find out the location of the celebration and second, get out of the village, without Zona or the village elders becoming suspicious.

Elves came and went everyday in the village but no matter how hard Gaea tried, they wouldn't let the location slip. Gaea decided to try and follow two of the elves that were preparing for the celebration. She hoped that since there were two of them they would be distracted enough not to notice her trailing them. Elves were so at home in the woods it would take all her skill and training to pull this off.

"I've seen them leaving before," Gaea told her sister. "I know they will go north out of the village and then turn at the large rock, toward the healing tree. You'll be hiding down that path on the right and I'll be on the left, that way one of us will be able to see the next turn."

"Okay," Naida said. "I'll help you, but I still think this is wrong. I like the elves and we shouldn't do anything to hurt them."

"I like them too," Gaea replied. "And I'm not going to hurt anyone. I just want to see what goes on in their ceremony. After all, they came to ours didn't they? So why is it so wrong for me to watch theirs?"

Naida and Gaea were good enough to do this and finally they found the clearing the elves were going to use. It was two days now, before the New Year and the girls would have to work fast to fix up a hiding place for Gaea. They also gathered leaves from the area so they could camouflage her clothes to blend in naturally with the surroundings. Finally, after a lot of preparation, Gaea was ready and not a moment too soon. The party was going to be tonight.

That night, right after supper Gaea feigned sickness and said she was going to bed early. Naida followed after her to make sure she was alright.

"Okay," Gaea said, "so far so good. Now, all we have to do is to sneak out of the house and out the gate, without anyone becoming suspicious. You'll need to come with me so you can close the gate behind me."

"Are you sure you want to go through with this?" Naida asked.

Gaea was dumbstruck. "Are you kidding? After all we've gone through to get this far, you think I'd quit now?"

"It's just that you know you're able to do it. Isn't that enough?" Naida asked.

"You saw the elves at our celebration; they just stood off to the side. They didn't get involved at all. I can't help but wonder what they do at their own ceremonies. Tonight I have the chance to find out, and you want me to stop?" Gaea asked.

"It's just that I really like the elves and I don't want to hurt them or make them mad." Naida replied. "They are very private about their lives and maybe we should respect that."

"I don't want to hurt them either." Gaea stated. "So let's make sure I don't get caught. That way, what they don't know, won't hurt us."

The girls slipped out of the house, while Zona and Larissa were in the kitchen, doing the dishes. They walked slowly toward the gate, hoping not to draw attention from anyone. As fate would have it, they ran into one of the village elders, Zorian.

"And what are you two doing out on a night like tonight?" Zorian asked "It's still a bit cool in the evenings, don't you agree?"

"Yes it is, sir." Gaea replied quickly. "I'm on my way to a friend's house to spend the night, and my sister was just walking along with me."

"Yeah," Naida continued. "It's alright, Zona knows all about it… Well, we should be on our way"

"Yes, yes, very good." Zorian said. "Yes, be on your way before you catch your death of cold."

The girls made it to the gate without any other encounters. Once Naida had let Gaea out, she headed back to the cottage before she was missed.

"Wait, wait," Gaea called out. "I forgot and left my ear-rings on the table. Can you put them back in my room for me?"

"Yeah, just keep it down," Naida replied, "before someone hears us."

Naida made it back home without any other trouble, but while she was slipping in Zona came in.

"What were you doing outside?" Zona asked.

"I was just getting a little fresh air. Do we have anymore of that cake?" Naida asked to change the subject.

"Yes, of course." Zona replied, always anxious to please.

Because of all this drama, Naida forgot all about Gaea's ear-rings. While she was eating her cake, Larissa found the ear-rings on the table. She had always admired them, but Gaea would never let her wear them. Now was her chance, as she was trying to get the last one in she dropped it. When it hit the floor, it shattered. Larissa was scared, she put them both back on the table and went into the kitchen. She had heard the word "cake" being mentioned.

Mean while, back at the clearing, Gaea was just about to her hiding place. There were elves all around the clearing and she had to be very careful not to be noticed. At last, she made it and not a moment too soon, the Elf Lords were forming a circle in the middle of the clearing and Chanook, The Prince, was in the center. The other elves were all gathered around. She had never seen so many elves at one time before.

Just as the ceremony was starting, she shifted to get a better view and the darkness shifted all around her. One of the elves close by noticed her and gave a shout. Immediately, she was surrounded and brought into the circle. Chanook recognized her right away.

"Why would you disgrace our ceremony like this?" Chanook asked. "You are a ring bearer and trying to become a master. I would expect better from you."

Gaea was ashamed, seeing the hurt in his eyes. "I'm so sorry. I hate that I have disappointed you. It's just that I love the elf people so much. I just wanted to know what went on here."

"If you love us so much, then respect our privacy." he stated.

"I understand now and I hope you can find it in your heart to forgive me." Gaea said, "I am ashamed by my actions and will never attempt to disgrace your ceremonies again."

Chanook agreed and let Gaea go. She was escorted to the village and helped back in. When she made it to the cottage, she slipped in and made it up to her room. Naida heard her come in and went to find out how it went.

"I really don't want to talk about it." Gaea said, "It didn't go well and I got caught. It was so embarrassing and Chanook was so disappointed too. I wish I could forget all about it for more than one reason. Have you ever felt darkness as a presence?"

"What do you mean?" Naida asked.

"When I was in my hiding place I could feel the darkness all around me like a presence and when I shifted it shifted too. That's why I got caught. I believe the darkness was trying to cause trouble with the elves and it used me for that purpose."

"That may be so," Naida agreed, "but it couldn't have done so without your participation."

"I know and that's what worries me." Gaea continued. "We would like to think that we are on the side of good but our actions betray us sometimes."

Then she noticed her ear-rings. "What happened to them?" Gaea asked

"I don't know." Naida answered. "Zona caught me coming in and I forgot all about them."

Larissa hearing them talking came into the room. "What's going on?"

"Do you know what happened to my ear-rings?" Gaea asked.

"I may have tried to put them on and dropped one." Larissa stammered, "But it's not my fault, if you hadn't left them out, or if Naida hadn't forgotten to put them up, I wouldn't have seen them. Besides, they must be cheap, if they break that easy. I don't know why you want to blame me."

About that time, there was a knock at the door. The girls headed down stairs just as Zona was opening the door. Gaea's heart skipped a beat, it was Zorian. He had come by to check on the girls, just to make sure they were alright. After Zona had heard his story, she thanked him and walked him to the door. Gaea was thinking…could this day get any worse?

"Now would you like to tell me just what's going on?" Zona asked as the girls came downstairs.

Gaea started at the beginning and told her the whole truth. When she finished, the silence was so thick you could almost slice it.

Zona finally spoke. "Before I decide the punishment, I would like to know if you have learned anything from all this?"

Gaea spoke up first. "Yes, I have. I've learned quite a bit actually. First, I learned that when you start lying, one thing leads to another and you have to keep on lying. Next, and probably more important, lying affects everybody around you. You really do hurt the ones you care the most about."

"Very good," Zona said, "And what about you two?"

"Well," Naida continued. "I've learned that if you lie to help another person, you are also guilty of lying. The truth is, if you help a person to do wrong, then you aren't really a friend to them."

"And you Larissa," Zona asked, "have you also learned anything?"

"Actually, I didn't have any part of all this." Larissa stated proudly. "But I have learned something. I now know that if you try to lay the blame on someone else, when you do something wrong, it's the same as lying. A person needs to take the responsibility for their own actions."

"Excellent," Zona exclaimed. "You may have made some terrible mistakes, but at least you've learned from them. I'm proud to say you have also earned your second ring…The Power of Truth. I hope you will use it wisely in the future."

"Now to the other matter," Zona continued, "I believe Gaea, you and Naida, should be grounded until the ceremony, and Larissa I think you should get Gaea a new pair of ear-rings like the ones you broke."

The time went quite fast, and soon it was time for the ring ceremony. The village people had the stage set up in the center of the village and the tables were spread with food fit for kings. Naida and Larissa were ready but Gaea wasn't quite so anxious this time, she dreaded seeing Chanook again.

After the rings were awarded, the party began. Most people had forgotten about the whole mess, but it was still strong in Gaea's mind. Then she saw the prince heading over.

"It's good to see you again, Gaea." Chanook said.

"I'm so glad you were able to make it, my Prince." Gaea replied. "I do hope you will accept my most humble apologies. I do regret my actions of late."

"Think nothing of it." Chanook answered. "You will make a fine Ring Master…one day. Until that time I will have to keep my eyes open, don't you think? Now, would you consider sitting at my table?" he asked with a smile.

"Of course, the pleasure would be mine." Gaea responded sweetly.

Parley, feint, jab, Gaea thought to herself, it's just like a dance. She could tell The Prince was funning with her, which she didn't mind at all. He was kind of cute.

The girls sang the night away. The first light of a new day was dawning in the east, as they made their way back to the cottage. They couldn't help but wonder how the next ring would come about.

TRUTH

To have the truth and never lie,
Is to live and never die.
A lie cuts deep, to the soul
And with those lies, never whole.
Live with lies and you will fall,
Continue there and lose it all.
To be one and live again,
You must first, remove that sin.
Know the truth; it'll set you free,
And there abide, eternally.

CHAPTER 4
HOPE

Ｗe find the girls in the middle of an argument. They'd just finished another lesson with Zona on their next ring, which would be Hope. They were true sisters, which mean they can't agree on anything.

"I don't care; I still hope that the elders will pick me to go on this village hunting trip." Naida said.

"But that's dumb," Gaea argued. "They already have everybody they need and they told you that maybe you could go next year."

"So, that doesn't mean that I can't hope to go this year. That's what hope is all about." Naida continued, "Besides, what great hope do you have?"

"I've already told you a thousand times." Gaea said, rolling her eyes upward. "I want to capture my own horse, when we go after the wild mustangs."

"Fat chance of that happening," Naida replied. "Nobody has ever gotten their own horse on the first trip."

"Yeah, well we'll just have to wait and see, won't we?" Gaea retorted.

"Hey! What about me?" Larissa asked.

"What about you?" Both Gaea and Naida asked together.

"Don't you guys want to know what I hope for?" Larissa asked unperturbed.

"NO!" They both said in unison, but laughed when they saw how shocked she looked.

As soon as they were able to stop laughing Gaea asked. "Ok, what is it that you hope for?"

But Larissa stuck her nose up in the air and said. "Huh, I'm not going to tell you now."

After a sufficient amount of pleading to find out, Larissa finally answered. "I hope for world peace. Don't start laughing again." Larissa said, stomping her foot. "It's a lot better than the dumb ole ideas you've got. Think about it, how good it would be if all the fighting would stop between humans, trolls, elves, and dwarfs."

"It's not that we are laughing at you." Naida said. "It's just that, that's impossible, it won't ever happen."

"Well, maybe so," Larissa agreed. "But isn't that, what hope's all about?"

Her sisters couldn't argue with that and the more they thought about it, the more they had to agree. *It would be a much better world if all the fighting would stop and all the races would work together. But that would never happen, would it?*

The next day was the last one before the hunt and round-up so Naida decided to go and check with the elders one last time, to see if she could go. On the way to find them she over heard two hunters talking; they were saying that the cook had fallen and broken his leg and wouldn't be able to go. She rushed to find the elders before they found someone else.

"Sirs, if I might have a moment of your time." Naida began. "I understand you've lost your cook on this excursion and I would like to offer my services. I'm a very good cook, I was taught by Zona."

Now most all the elders have eaten at Zona's, at one time or another and they all knew how good a cook she was, so they replied. "We know that you've wanted to go on this hunt. Now you understand you would be the cook; you won't be allowed to hunt."

"Kind sirs, I must admit that I would like very much to be able to hunt, but this situation suits me just fine." Naida responded, and thinking about Larissa added quickly. "Would it be possible for me to bring my sister as an assistant? She would be a tremendous help and is also an excellent cook."

"We'll check with Zona, if it's alright with her, then you both may go." they replied. "But remember, you're going as the cook and nothing else."

"Great! You won't regret it." Naida said, before running off to find Larissa.

That night, as the girls were all preparing to leave in the morning, Gaea still couldn't believe that Naida had pulled it off. "You may be going, but you won't be able to hunt."

"I know, but that's good enough for this year, at least I'll be allowed to go. Next year, though, hopefully I'll be able to hunt. Besides, I was just hoping to be able to go and now I am."

"Yeah," Gaea replied, "I guess I'm glad. It'll be good having you along and the food will be a lot better. 'Ole Joe' didn't think it was done unless it was burnt."

Naida asked Larissa, "You don't mind going as my assistant, do you?"

"Are you kidding?" She responded. "I'll be the youngest person to ever go on one of these hunts. That'll kind of make me famous, huh?"

They all laughed as they got ready for bed. It was going to be a busy day tomorrow.

The hunt had been going on for three days and everything was going great. The hunt was a big success and there was going to be plenty of meat for the winter. Even Gaea had brought in two big bucks. The other hunters were proud of her; it was unusual for anyone to do that good on their first hunt. The food had been excellent and no one had been hurt. The way things were going; this could be the best hunt ever.

Tomorrow they were going to try for the horses. If they could trap enough to trade with the other villages it would be perfect. The day dawned bright and clear. The hunters had already picked the blind canyon to use as the trap. They would drive the herd into the canyon and, since there was no other way out, they would catch the horses one at a time.

The party set out early the next morning, while Naida and Larissa were still cleaning up after breakfast. The girls were planning a special feast for the last night of the hunt. They were going to the river for some water when Larissa got stuck in a big mud hole. If Naida hadn't been there, she probably wouldn't have gotten out. Naida had run back and gotten a rope from camp to pull her out.

When the girls finally made it to the river, they decided to go for a swim and wash off. They hadn't been swimming long, when they heard an awful commotion back over the hill. They got out and headed in the direction of all the commotion. When they reached the top of the hill, they found a small pony trapped in the same mud hole that Larissa had been caught in.

They ran down and Naida made a halter out of the rope they had with them. After they got it over his head, they were able to use it to pull the pony out. He was bucking and jumping like crazy until Larissa came over to him and put a hand on his head. He immediately calmed down They led him back to the river, washed off again, and got the water they needed then headed back to camp.

"Where did you learn that?" Naida asked.

"I really don't know." Larissa answered. "It just seemed like the thing to do. I could tell he was scared and unsure of our intentions."

"Sometimes you're weird." Naida responded. "But in a good way."

Meanwhile, at the canyon, Gaea and the others were rounding up the horses and driving them into the dead end. Once they had them enter the bottleneck, they blocked off the exit with logs that had been cut for that purpose. Then it was just a matter of time before they could get a rope on and string them together. There were about thirty horses in the canyon now and it was time to start gathering them in.

The ropers would walk among the herd, pick out the horse they were after, and then lasso him. At this point, the fight would begin, and was just a matter of being able to hold on until the fight was out of him. Gaea had mastered any weapon that she picked up but the rope would be the death of her. Most of the time, she would tie herself up while trying to swirl it over her head, the other times she roped a tree, a rock, and one time another roper. She gave the others plenty to laugh about which made most of them feel a lot better, since she usually made them look silly with weapons training. One time she actually got the rope on a horse but before she could get her feet planted it took off, needless to say, with her dragging behind. She finally had to cut it loose and accept not getting a horse today.

Everyone was surprised to find the girls had caught a pony. They could hardly believe that the girls could have made such a delicious feast and found the time to catch a pony too. It would be a long time before anyone forgot this hunting trip. The hunters decided the Woodland girls were a good luck charm and should be allowed to come on all the hunts in the future.

"I'm so sore," Gaea said as they sat around the campfire. "I hurt in places that I didn't even know I had."

"Here try this," Naida said, handing her a very smelly concoction wrapped in leaves. "Rub this on the muscles that hurt."

"What is it?" Gaea asked reluctantly.

"It's a mixture of Wolf's bane." Naida stated flatly.

"Are you crazy?" Gaea cried, while jumping backwards. "That stuff is poisonous."

"Relax sis." Naida replied with a smile. "In its diluted form it makes a great paste to help heal sore muscles. Try it; you'll be glad you did."

The next morning Gaea did feel much better but it didn't help her at all when it came to catching a horse. That day was pretty much a repeat of the day before. After all the horses were caught up and tied together the villagers decided to leave them in the canyon for the night. It would be safer and they could come and get them in the morning when they were leaving. They left two guards and headed back to camp after a very successful day.

When the girls arrived back in Truitt, Zona was waiting, anxious to hear all about their hunting trip. After hearing about Naida and Larissa's pony and Gaea's nearly catching her horse, and all the tidbits that went on, she asked what they had learned.

"Well," Gaea started, "I've learned that you don't always get what you hope for, no matter how hard you might try, but that doesn't change it because I still hope to get a horse next year."

"That's very good Gaea," Zona replied, smiling, "and what about you girls? Did you learn anything also?"

"I sure did," Naida jumped in. "I learned that you can't just sit around and wait on what you're hoping for. You have to do everything in your power to get what you want."

"Well, I learned something too," Larissa continued. "I've learned that sometimes you can get things you never even dreamed of hoping for, like getting to go on this trip or our pony. And there are some hopes that have to be shared by everybody before they'll ever come true."

"Excellent." Zona replied, beaming with pride. "I couldn't have said it better myself. I hope you never forget these lessons and that all your hopes will eventually come to pass, like earning another ring. Congratulations."

"Yeah," Larissa said. "This time Gaea, you won't have to be embarrassed around the elves."

"You mean around Prince Chanook don't you?" Naida asked.

"That's enough you two," Zona said. "Things in the past should stay in the past."

"Yeah, but Gaea wants Prince Chanook in her future too," Naida teased.

Gaea made a grab at her sister but missed just as she took off running. "Just wait till I get my hands on you. You'll be lucky to have a future when I get through with you." Gaea yelled and started to chase after her.

Larissa and Zona both started laughing as they watched them run out of sight. World peace might be easier to accomplish than for her sisters to get along without fighting. The celebration was great… good food, good company, and plenty of music. After Zona gave the girls their new ring, Prince Chanook gave them another surprise.

The elves made special gifts for each of the girls. Gaea received an elfin traveling cloak, which was great for camouflaging. It would blend into the surroundings no matter what it was, with the understanding not to use it to sneak into elfin ceremonies. Naida received an elfin long bow. She was pretty good with a bow already but with this bow she could shoot further and more accurate. Larissa was good with thrown weapons like the knife. She could hit a moving target at forty paces every time, so they gave her their very best spear. It was light weight and more durable than any she had ever seen.

After presenting the gifts Prince Chinook said, "I need to talk with all of you. Your mother was very special to me."

Gaea interrupted him, "You knew our mother? Why didn't you tell us?" Gaea demanded.

"Your impatience is very disturbing. It is enough to try the patience of the mountains." Chanook replied, biting his tongue.

"What do you mean the patience of the mountains?" Naida interjected.

"In the far west there are trees that grow so big it takes half a days' journey to walk around the trunk. Sequoias, they live ten of my lifetimes. It is said that the mountains watch the Sequoia grow and the trees watch the mountains erode into hills. Even with all this time, your impatience would destroy both trees and mountains. Now I'm trying to tell you, if you could try to be silent for just a moment." Chanook continued. "Yes, I knew your mother. In fact, I was there the day you were born, Gaea."

"I can't believe you've never told me this before." Gaea stated in disbelief. "After all this time and you never said anything about knowing my mother and father. You did know him too, I suppose?"

"Yes, I knew him well." Chanook replied, rolling his eyes toward the ceiling. You humans never cease to amaze me. You rush around, worrying about this or that, so intent on getting every moment of every day."

"Well, we don't have ten lifetimes to get things done. We have to do it in just one." Gaea replied.

"Yes. Well, I guess that is what I like most about you; your intensity of life. We may live for ten of your lifetimes in years but we differ in others ways too." Chanook was going to continue when he was interrupted again.

"Differ in other ways? What other ways? What do you mean we differ in other ways?" Gaea asked, astonished.

The Prince continued once again. "Well, for starters, we only have one child in our lifetime. All our hopes and dreams rely on just one heir. Now, before you interrupt again, your mother was very special to me because my daughter died to save her life. Do you understand what that means? My one heir died so your mother could continue to live her very short existence. In some ways that makes you and your sisters my heirs also."

"I'm so sorry to hear that." Gaea stammered. "Where? When? Uh, why? Forget that; is there anything that we can do?"

"I don't believe I've ever seen you lost for words, Gaea." Chanook smiled. "It was before you were born; your father was still Captain of the Guards in the castle. I believe it was one of the many reasons he resigned his post."

"We were visiting the castle at a time when some assassins were trying to kill the king. My daughter, Celeste, and your mother were in the outer chamber when they broke in. Celeste jumped in front of an arrow meant for your mother. The attack was over in a matter of minutes but it was too late for Celeste." Chanook spoke quietly and took a moment to gather himself. "Your father hunted them down and killed them all, before the sun set that day, but it couldn't help Celeste. She died in my arms before morning."

"The reason I'm telling you this now," the Prince continued, "is the darkness is growing stronger and I worry about you. I believe the darkness took my daughter but it wanted your mother to prevent your births. I believe your existence is crucial to our future and the darkness has tried several times to stop you. So far it has been unsuccessful but it's growing stronger."

"We'll be careful Prince." Gaea answered. "The time will come that we will get our revenge on the darkness and whoever is behind it."

"Yeah," Naida added.

"Me too," Larissa chimed in.

The Prince agreed, "Yes I do believe you will. Just remember, there's more riding on this than just your revenge."

The girls thanked the Prince and all the elves for the gifts and headed to Zona's. They had much to think about on the way. Sooner or later, there was going to be a showdown. The girls just hoped that they would be ready.

HOPE

Without hope, big or small,
Life wouldn't mean much at all.
So never give up hopes or your dreams,
No matter how silly or impossible they seem.

CHAPTER 5
KNOWLEDGE

I t had been several years since the girls first came to Truitt and they had become an important part of the society there. We find the girls preparing for a trip to the Salt Flat. Salt is one thing that can't be grown or produced, it has to be found. The Salt Flat is an area, at the base of Mount Arrack, which had an abundance of salt. It just needed to be sifted out of the sand. It's not that difficult to do, it just takes a while to get there, and a dragon had been sighted in the area.

The girls volunteered for this duty for two reasons. One, they wanted to get out of the village for a while, and two, they hated this dragon. They knew it was one of the ones that killed their father, by the smell of its dragon-fire. This dragon belonged to a wicked witch called, Broom-rider. They felt she was an enemy to all that was good, especially to people that wear the Rings of Power and they believed that she was the source of the darkness that was invading the land.

"I sure hope we run across that dragon." Gaea said.

"Me too," Naida added. "I've got special arrows just for it."

"Yeah," Larissa continued. "I need to see how my new spear works out."

"How did you become so good with thrown weapons, anyway?" Gaea asked.

"When we were traveling with Gar, I couldn't get over how good he was at throwing rocks," Larissa said. "I figured if he could be that good with rocks, I should be able to do it with knives. He showed me how to concentrate on nothing but what I was doing. It's like becoming one with the knife."

"Yeah, that's what it's like with the sword," Gaea replied. "It becomes a part of you, an extension of your arm, and the more graceful the dance, the more dangerous the blow."

"We need to get going," Naida interrupted, "if we're ever going to get there."

The girls had Sam, their donkey, packed up with their supplies. Normally they would carry it themselves, but they needed the donkey to carry the salt back. They needed to get enough to make it worthwhile for going. The girls headed south, it was a two day trip to get to Mount

Arrack, and the girls were anxious to get there, hoping to find more than just salt.

They traveled long after dark and set up a dry camp that night; no fire, no tent. They just ate jerky that night. Early the next morning, it was time to move on and they were determined to get there as soon as possible. A few hours before sunset they arrived at the Salt Flat. They had plenty of time left to set up camp. This time they went all out, set up their tents, hauled water up from the creek, chopped firewood, and stacked it up close by. Perfect, they thought, surely this would attract the dragon. The girls cooked a big meal that night, but instead of going to bed afterwards they hid themselves in the rocks close by, waiting and hoping to meet the dragon that killed their father.

Needless to say, the dragon never showed. The whole night was wasted waiting and nothing to show for it. Now, as tired as they were, they needed to start collecting salt. Salting was really very easy. First, you had to wash down the sand, this let the water absorb the salt out of the sand. Then you set the water in the sun to let it evaporate, this left pure salt in the container. The girls worked past noon before stopping to eat.

"If we keep up this pace," Larissa said, "we'll have enough in a few days."

"Yeah," Naida replied, "that'll give us plenty of time to track down that dragon if it doesn't show up first."

"Well," Gaea said, "we definitely need to come up with another plan for our nights. We can't all stay up every night. We'll have to take turns keeping watch."

"We sure do, but I just knew it would come the first night," Naida said. "Why don't you get some rest now, Gaea? That way, you can take the first watch, and Larissa and I will continue collecting salt."

"That sounds good to me." Gaea agreed.

Nothing happened that night or the next two. The girls would finish getting the salt they needed the next day, and they were worried the dragon wouldn't show. They were talking that night about their teachings.

Lately Zona had been teaching the different types of knowledge. There was intelligence, then being smart, and lastly wisdom.

Intelligence is learned out of books, while being smart is learned from life, and wisdom is absorbed from your surroundings. Zona explained it like this-- 2 + 2 =? Answers: A) 1 B) 4 C) 122. An intelligent person would know the answer is 4. A smart person would add the two and find out the answer is 4. A wise person would look at the answers and deduce- 1 is less than the numbers added so it has to be wrong, and 122 is a three digit number and you can't get a three digit answer by adding two single digit numbers, so 4 must be the correct answer.

It was during their discussion that the dragon struck. He didn't attack them though. He took their donkey. Without him, they couldn't get the salt back to the village. That was just one more reason to go after it. The girls started making plans to track it down, but how do you track something that doesn't leave tracks?

Now, of the three girls, Gaea was the intelligent one and Naida was the smart one, and even though Larissa was the youngest, she was the wisest.

"I've read stories about Broom-rider and all agree that she lives at the top of Mount Arrack, so it stands to reason, that is where the dragon would go." Gaea said.

"I agree," Naida said. "We'll need to make some ropes out of vines. They'll be a big help when climbing the mountain."

The girls slept fitful that night, they rose early to start making preparations. They wanted to start climbing by noon. Gaea and Naida noticed that Larissa seemed to be daydreaming a bit more than usual today. Little did they know that she was trying to make sense of the dream she had last night. *She dreamed of a golden dragon holding an egg. She could not imagine what that would mean, but she couldn't get it out of her head.* Finally, everything was ready; they decided to eat a good meal before setting out.

Gaea led the way, since she was the most experienced at climbing which meant she had read about it in a book somewhere. They followed a trail about halfway up the mountain and then they had to start climbing. It turns out that Larissa was the best at scaling the mountain. She was like a little monkey when it came to climbing. She would go up first and then drop down the rope so her sisters could climb up. They continued to leap frog like this until they finally reached the top. It was close to dark by now, so they decided to set up a dry camp, until they could check their surroundings in the morning.

That night, while on watch, Gaea noticed a light way off in the distance. That must be where Broom-rider lives, she thought. She knew that Broom-rider must have sent the dragon after her father, but she also knew that she, herself, was no match for that witch, at least not yet. One day that witch would get what was coming to her, but for now Gaea would settle for the dragon.

Gaea knew from her studies and reading that dragons liked to live in caves, so they were watching for any indication of the dragon's whereabouts as they traveled. Naida happened to notice buzzards circling in the distance. That must be where its cave was located. The buzzards were looking for some left-overs, hopefully it wasn't Sam. As the girls got closer, the smell got stronger; this had to be the dragon's lair.

"Let's go in one at a time," Gaea suggested. "That way, we can't all get caught in a trap. Have your weapons at the ready, and your eyes open. I'll go first because I can use my travel cloak to help hide, then you Naida and Larissa will protect our backs."

The girls made their way deep into the cave, and finally came upon the dragon's lair. They searched the area thoroughly. There was no sign of their donkey but they did find a nest with one egg in it.

"It has to be the dragon's egg." Gaea said.

"Yeah, let's break it." Naida added.

"No," Larissa said, thinking about her dream. "Let's keep it, it may come in handy. We can use it to lure the dragon into a trap or we can swap it for Sam."

"Good idea," Naida agreed. "We can always destroy it later if we need to."

Larissa put the egg in her pack and they headed back to the surface. They hadn't traveled far, when all of a sudden, the cave floor fell out from under them and they slid down deep into the mountain. When they finally came to a stop, they found some torches and started looking around. There didn't seem to be a way out. The walls seemed solid all the way around, except for one area. Naida noticed the smoke from the torch filtered into the wall.

"There has to be a secret doorway here," Naida stated. "See the way the smoke disappears into the rocks. Look around for some kind of a switch to make it open."

"Here it is!" Gaea exclaimed, as she pulled on a torch holder mounted on the wall of the cave.

The wall opened up and revealed a path leading up toward the surface. The girls followed with weapons in hand, until they reached another large cavern. There was a strange two-headed beast on the far side. As they made their way closer to the beast, they heard Broom-rider's voice calling down from above.

"Welcome to my mountain." she screeched. "May I introduce you to my beast of choice? You see, one of the heads always lies; the other head always tells the truth. The problem is deciding which is which. This should not be a problem for you, since you have the ring for the Power of Choice.

Before you are two doors, one door leads to safety; the other to certain destruction. You may ask only one question of the beast to help you in your decision. Choose wisely."

Broom-rider left, knowing that no one had ever beaten her beast. You see, a person must know which door is correct. The consequences are too severe to simply guess. The girls talked it over among themselves for a while.

"If we just ask which door to choose, we won't know if the answer is the truth or a lie." Gaea stated.

"Yeah, and if we ask a question to determine which tells the truth, then we've used our only question." Naida added.

"I've got it!" Larissa exclaimed, as she walked toward the beast.

"Which door will the other head tell us to choose?" She asked the head on the left.

"The door on the right." the beast answered.

"Then we will choose the door on the left." Larissa stated.

Gaea and Naida looked at her, still not understanding what that proved, but before they could ask Larissa explained. "Don't you see? No matter which head we ask, the answer it gives is going to be a lie. If the head on the left tells the truth and I ask that question, the answer he gives is going to be a lie because that is what the other head would tell us. If the head on the left lies, then it's the same thing, the other head would tell us the truth but this head has to lie, so the answer is still going to a lie."

Her sisters were amazed, but they had to agree that she was right. They opened the door on the left and walked through. Once inside they heard the floor at the other door open up. If they had chosen that door, they would have dropped to a fiery death.

They followed the path upward only to be met by the dragon. Well, at least it wasn't...certain death. Larissa reached into her pack and withdrew the egg. The dragon recognized it immediately, as she raised it over her head.

Now, dragons can't talk but they can communicate using pictures or images in the mind. Larissa had gotten pretty good at this. She was showing this dragon an image of them trading the egg for their donkey. The dragon nodded agreement and allowed them to walk out on the plains of the Salt Flat. She took flight and returned in moments with Sam, their donkey, unhurt but hungry. Larissa mentally transmitted one more picture, one where the dragon and the girls were fighting. The dragon understood, the next time they met, there would be a battle, but for now they would each go their own way.

The girls finished gathering the salt they needed and packed up ready to leave in the morning, after Sam had supper and a good nights' sleep. Naida took this opportunity to gather another substance she had found useful. Sulfur, it was a yellow powder usually found around areas of salt. She needed to restock her supply. You never know when you might need a good stink bomb.

The return trip to Truitt was uneventful and gave the girls time to enjoy being in woods again. On the trip down they were so concerned with revenge that they failed to remember why they loved the woods so much. The world was a wonderful place if you just take the time to enjoy it.

The first night while Larissa was on watch, she realized that the voices she kept hearing were the animals in the woods. She wondered if her sisters were able to hear the animals like she could. She was afraid to ask because they always made fun of her. She decided to wait and ask Zona about it because this wasn't the first time.

When they reached Truitt, they turned the salt over to the elders, and went to find Zona. They could hardly wait to tell her of their adventures.

After hearing the story, Zona asked. "Well, that's a mighty fine story, that's for sure, but did you learn anything?"

"You bet we did," Gaea replied. "We were talking about our lessons on knowledge but this experience let us learn first hand what the lessons were all about. I may be the most intelligent but it takes more than intellect in most situations."

"Yeah," Naida added. "Gaea may have known where to go and I was smart enough to make the ropes to get us there, but it was Larissa's wisdom that got us out of there alive."

"It's not one over the other though," Larissa continued. "It's a combination of intellect, smarts, and wisdom to solve a problem. It takes all three to make a complete person."

"Exactly," Zona said. "That's just what I needed to hear from all of you. Not only did you get the salt we needed, but you've earned your next ring, the Power of Knowledge. Remember though, an intelligent person opens his mouth, a smart person opens his ears and mouth, and a wise person opens his ears."

"Yes we know," Gaea said. "An intelligent person tells what he knows.'

"And a smart person listens and tells what is needed," Naida added.

"But a wise person listens," Larissa finished. "Because he knows, there is something he can learn from everyone."

"Excellent, I look forward to presenting this ring." Zona stated proudly.

The girls were excited about getting their next ring. This meant they were well on their way to becoming a Ring Master and also there will be another party.

"I'll get to see Chanook again," Gaea said.

"Yeah and the other elves," Naida added.

"And food," Larissa said. "Don't forget about the food."

The girls laughed as they made their way to the cottage. It would be good to sleep in a bed again. They loved the woods but the comforts of home were pretty good too. As they walked Larissa slowed down to walk with Zona.

"Grand-ma," she asked slowly, 'Is it possible to talk to animals."

"Yes, my dear." Zona answered. "It is very possible if you have the magic and evidently you do."

"Do you think my sisters can talk to them too?" Larissa asked.

"No, I don't think so." Zona replied. "I don't sense the magic in them like I do you. Each Ring Master develops a special talent. Yours seems to be magic, Naida is going to be chemistry I believe, and Gaea's will probably be the use of weapons."

"I'm glad I'm not going crazy." Larissa said as she ran to catch up with her sisters.

CHAPTER 6
HONESTY

The village of Truitt was bustling with the news that Princess Sara would be coming to the Harvest of the Full Moon. Everybody was hurrying around trying to get everything perfect for her visit. Zelda, the inn-keeper, was busy getting the Royal Suite ready for her stay. The Royal Suite was really just a regular room but it had a connecting door so both rooms together made it a suite. Zelda had enlisted the aid of Naida and Larissa to help clean and prepare the rooms.

The girls had never met a real Princess before, the closest they'd come was meeting Prince Chanook of the elves. But this was a real human Princess, complete with castle and king and all the trimmings. They were just finishing up, and they still had to head back to Zona's to help clean and to do their lessons. They were learning the difference between truth and honesty. They had the Ring of Truth, but Zona was saying they needed to work on the Ring of Honesty now.

Naida and Larissa were headed back to the cottage, when they came up on Bud, the son of one of the elders. Bud was selling tickets to see the Princess to anyone that would listen to him. The girls knew that no one needed a ticket to see her and they told him so.

"Bud, you need to quit cheating these people," Naida said. "You know that this isn't right."

"I'm not cheating anyone," Bud replied sharply. "Everybody with one of my tickets WILL be able to see the Princess, so what's wrong with that?"

Larissa jumped in, "Yes, they will be able to see the Princess but they don't need your ticket to do it, though."

"Well, it's not my fault if the people don't know that," Bud replied. "I haven't lied."

It was at that moment, both Naida and Larissa realized what Zona was talking about. Bud was telling the truth. The people with his ticket will be able to see the Princess but what he was doing was still dishonest. There was a big difference between truth and honesty.

"Bud, I'm not going to stand here and argue with you. You need to give these people their money back and you need to do it now." Naida stated flatly. "If you don't tell them the truth then I will."

"You have no right to do that," Bud yelled, his face turning red. "If you do, I'll tell my daddy and you'll be in big trouble."

"Excuse me, folks." Larissa hollered. "May I have your attention please? I believe you may have been misled, you don't need a ticket to be able to see the Princess."

Naida and Larissa smiled as the people he had cheated ran back over demanding their money back. Bud was fuming. Naida had hoped that he would have confessed on his own, but it had to be done anyway. The girls had to run. Zona would be wondering what had happened to them, and they really didn't want her to know about this. Bud probably would cause trouble over this before it was over. His daddy was an elder and held a high position in the village.

The girls got to the cottage just as Zona was looking out the door. They rushed on in and started cleaning before she could ask any questions. Zona kept her house clean all the time but she wasn't sure if the Princess would come over while she was visiting this trip. Zona had been the teacher for the Princess too. It surprised the girls to learn that Princess Sara was a Ring Master, which was why she was going to be the Master of Ceremonies tomorrow night at the festival.

Tonight, though, there was going to be a big dinner at the inn in her honor. Everybody was invited but only the big-wigs, like the chief, village elders, Zona, and of course Princess Sara

would sit at the main table. The girls had promised Zelda that they would help serve but what they really wanted was to be able to meet the Princess.

Gaea lucked out to be one of the hunters, to help get game for the feast tonight and tomorrow but it was time for her to be getting home. They had to leave soon, to go to the inn and finish getting the meal ready.

"It's about time. Where have you been?" Naida asked Gaea as she walked in the door.

"Hunting, but you know that." she answered. "Why? What's up?"

"We've got to get going. I'll tell you on the way." Naida replied, and then told Gaea all about Bud on the way to the inn.

"He's such a brat," Gaea said as Naida finished. "He probably will try and cause trouble."

The girls went to work cooking and setting the tables for the dinner. Everything was almost ready when Zona came in and called Naida and Larissa into another room.

"I've just had a long talk with Bud's father," Zona said. "Now, I would like to hear your side of this story, before I decide what to do. Is this true? Did you make him lose all that money?"

"Yes, it's true," Larissa mumbled, "but what he was doing was wrong. He didn't have any right to cheat those people like that."

"That's right, grandma." Naida continued. "He was wrong, and if we'd have let him get away with it…well, it's like we would have been a part of it if we hadn't done something. We did it and I'm afraid that we would do it again if we had to."

"Well, we don't have time to get into this now," Zona said. "I'll talk to you both later. The Princess has arrived and you still have more work to do."

Everything was ready when the guests started arriving. The girls escorted each one to their tables and seated them. When everyone was seated the Princess made her entrance. She stood in the doorway until every eye was focused on her. She was just a little over 5 foot tall but her presence filled the whole room. She seemed to glide as she made her way around the room greeting each and every guest as if they were her very best friend. Her smile was quick and lit up the whole room and in no time at all everyone felt completely at ease in her presence.

Zelda was pleased at the way the girls behaved around the Princess. They stood by ready to serve or aid the guests in any way possible, and were prompt with each course of the meal. Everything went without a hitch. Princess Sara complimented Zelda on her dinner and the accommodations.

After the dinner, the girls were cleaning up and noticed Zona and the Princess talking in private. They probably had a lot of catching up to do. It had been a long time since Zona had seen Sara. The girls could hardly believe how sweet the Princess was. She was so polite and proper in everything she did. She acted like a regular person.

While Gaea was sweeping up around the tables, she noticed something lying on the floor. As she picked it up, she realized it was a necklace. It must belong to the Princess. It was so beautiful. This would make a great memento to remember this night forever. The Princess would probably never miss it anyway. Gaea slipped it in her pocket, while looking around to see if anyone had noticed her.

By the time the girls got to the cottage it was late, so everyone went straight to bed. Gaea was tired but she couldn't get to sleep. She kept thinking about the necklace. *She wanted to keep it so badly, not because it was valuable but because it belonged to a real Princess. She would never get another opportunity like this again but she knew in her heart that she would have to give it back.* Once she decided that she went right to sleep.

Gaea awoke early the next morning, and left before anyone else was up. She was hoping to talk to the Princess before anyone found out. As she walked in the door of the inn, Sara was coming down the stairs, into the main dinning area. Gaea walked up and bowed deeply.

"Excuse me, your Majesty." Gaea began slowly. "I believe I may have something of yours. I found it on the floor last night."

"OH YES!" Sara exclaimed, as Gaea pulled the necklace out. "I've looked everywhere for this. It was a present from my mother and it means the world to me. I'm glad you're so honest and were willing to return it to me."

"Well, to tell you the truth," Gaea stammered. "I was tempted to keep it. I'm so sorry I let you worry all night. If I'd known you were up, I would have brought it back last night."

"Think nothing of it." Sara said. "I'm just glad to have it back."

"Well, if you will excuse me, I must be getting back." Gaea requested, hoping that no one would have noticed her absence.

When she arrived back at Zona's, her sisters were just coming down stairs and Zona was in the kitchen finishing breakfast. She walked on in and started setting the table, as her sisters poured the drinks. Nobody was the wiser. They didn't have to find out.

Just as the girls were finished washing the dishes, there was a knock at the door. It was Princess Sara; she was going for a ride and was here to invite Zona and the girls to accompany her. Zona thought that it was an excellent idea, and quickly packed a picnic to take with them.

It had been a good while since the girls had been horse-back riding, and it was good to get away from the hustle and bustle of the preparations for the Harvest Festival. As the girls galloped and frolicked, Zona and Sara were able to catch up on old times. A little after noon they all gathered in a clearing beside a quite, peaceful lake.

"Well, girls," Princess Sara began. "I'm so glad you agreed to come with us. It will give us a chance to get to know each other."

"There's nothing we'd like more, your Highness." Gaea said.

"Please, please, call me Sara." she began, "At least, when we are alone, anyway. I've been meaning to tell you how sorry I was to hear about your father."

"Did you know him?" Naida asked.

"Oh, yes," Sara answered. "He was the Captain of the Guard, for my father."

"Wow!" Larissa exclaimed. "He never talked about that at all. Why did he quit? Do you know?"

"He left while I was still a young girl but from what I understand, he quit so you girls would be raised in the Woodlands," Sara replied. "It seems he didn't think the palace was any place to be raising kids. My father said Beltar wasn't much for the politics and double dealing that goes on, sometimes."

"I can't imagine what life would have been like in the castle." Gaea said.

"Well, you probably would be some of my Maids in Waiting." Sara replied, "They are unmarried ladies, waiting on a proper suitor."

"Nothing personal, but I don't believe I'd be waiting on any man."

Gaea answered, starting to turn red. "I can get along just fine by myself."

"Yes, I do believe, your father made the right decision," Sara added.

Gaea continued, "I'm glad that we have been able to get to know you, though. You're so sweet and polite, even to regular people like us."

"It has been a pleasure to get to know all of you, and I hope we can become good friends. That's one of the problems of life in the castle; you don't know who you can really trust. And with this darkness spreading across the kingdom, it's frightful to think of all the things that could happen." Sara said.

"Well, you can sure trust us," Naida said and all the girls agreed. "If there is ever, anything you need, all you have to do is ask."

"That is most reassuring and the same goes for me. If there is anything I can do for you please let me know." Sara responded.

"I do believe it must be time to head back," Zona said.

It was a pleasant ride back to Truitt. As the Princess stopped by the inn, the girls continued on to their cottage. It was about time to start getting ready, and the girls were excited, talking about their new friend, Sara. Wow, it was unbelievable to think about having a real Princess, as a friend.

Everybody was arriving, Chanook and the elves, Gar was strolling by, people from the surrounding area, all were making their way to the court square. It was going to be the best festival ever and all because the Princess was going to be heading the festivities.

As everybody gathered around, Princess Sara stood in the center of the square with Zona and Chief Goridon. After Goridon had gotten everybody's attention he took his seat. Zona then gave the Princess two rings and she also took her seat. Sara then told the story of Bud, Naida, and Larissa.

"All evil needs to succeed, is for good people to do nothing." Princess Sara spoke to the crowd. "I am proud to say that in Truitt, you have good people who are willing to do what is necessary. Would Naida and Larissa please come up here?"

As the girls made there way into the center the Princess continued. "Naida and Larissa, I am honored to award you your next Ring of Power, the ring of Honesty. I hope that you will never allow evil to exist without a fight."

"Now if I may, would Gaea please come up?" Sara called out.

As Gaea made her way to the center, the Princess told the audience the story of the necklace that she had lost.

"Gaea, it is rare to find this kind of honesty in the world today. I am glad to present you with this Ring of Honesty." Sara proclaimed as she pulled the ring off her finger to place it on Gaea's. "I am equally proud to call you my friend."

"I present to you all; Gaea, Naida, and Larissa, bearers of the Rings of Power. I hope you know, Truitt, how lucky you are."

The crowd erupted in a deafening round of applause that lasted for several minutes. When it finally quieted down a bit the Princess proclaimed. "Let the festivities began!"

The celebration lasted long into the night. Gaea made the introductions between Chinook, the elf Prince, and Princess Sara, and they all sang and laughed and then ate some more. The Woodland girls decided this was the best party ever, and could not imagine how it could possibly get any better than this.

CHAPTER 7
LOVE

Naida stormed into the cottage, "I think I could ring his neck. Aarg! I'm so mad I could bite nails. Who does he think he is?"

"Is something wrong?" Gaea asked, knowing that Naida's boyfriend, Ben, had broken up with her.

"No, well… no. Yes. I don't know," Naida stammered. "I'm just so mad I can't see straight. The nerve of some people. How could he?"

Naida finally broke down and cried. Gaea came over and put her arm around her, gave her a hug, and just held her. "Why doesn't he still love me?" Naida asked between sobs.

"Because he's a jerk," Gaea answered. "He doesn't know what he wants. You're better off without him, anyway."

"I loved him though," Naida whined. "What's wrong with me? Why would Ben say he doesn't love me anymore?"

"I told you. HE'S… A… JERK. He's making a play for that girl in the next village, like she's going to give him the time of day. He's out for conquests and you wouldn't give in, so he's looking else where. That's all there is to it. You're better off without him." Gaea finished.

About that time, Zona walked in. "Everything okay, girls?"

"Yeah," Naida said. "Grandma, when you first started talking about the Ring of Love, I thought this would be the easiest of them all…but love hurts, it hurts really badly."

"Yes, I know." Zona replied, "It may not seem like it, but things will get better."

"I'm going to be real good at this ring," Larissa said, coming into the room, "Because I love everybody."

"Yes, well, do you love everybody the same?" Zona asked.

"Well, no," Larissa stammered. "I guess I don't."

"And Naida," Zona continued, "Do you remember how happy you were, when you first started liking this boy? How much fun it was just to be together?"

"Yes, I guess so." Naida answered slowly, wondering if this was a trick question.

"That will happen again," Zona said, smiling. "Just you wait and see. Love will come a calling, that's for sure. It's all part of growing up."

"Gaea, do you remember your cat Cleopatra?" Zona asked. "Do you remember how hurt you were, when she died?"

"Sure," Gaea replied. "It hurt really badly and I kept wondering, why did my cat have to die? She was the most civilized cat in the whole world. It hurt a lot back then but now, I miss her but it's the good times I remember."

"Exactly, sometimes love hurts but it's the good times we remember, when we look back." Zona agreed. "And those good times are what make love worthwhile."

"Well, all I know is, this love stuff sure is complicated." Naida said.

"Yes it is." Zona agreed. "There's more to it than that, too. Sometimes, your boy-friend may try and talk you into something you really don't want to do. Many times, your friends will also try to influence you to do something wrong. The thing to remember is this: if he is the one and he really loves you, he won't mind waiting and friends that want you to do something wrong, really aren't your friends."

"Well," Gaea asked, "do we know enough now to get our ring?"

"Oh my, no" Zona replied, laughing. "There is so much more to learn. There are different types of love; like boy-friend, family, friends, strangers, and even enemies. Did you know that most of the trouble in this world today is because of love or hate? Love affects everything in your lives, from what you do, to where you go, and even how you feel. There is much more to understand before you can earn the ring. If you really want to earn the ring, then maybe you should go through the Forbidden Woods."

The Forbidden Woods was a very dangerous place and it is inhabited by trolls. Trolls have nothing, what-so-ever, to do with people. They wished people didn't exist; they didn't like them, and hoped to never see one. This is the place that the girls were going to pass through… hopefully.

It was a two day trek just to get to the Forbidden Woods, so early the next morning the girls were packed and ready to go. Zona gave them a map showing the safest path through the forest and waved good-bye as they disappeared into the trees.

Things were going pretty good until the second day. Gaea was scouting up ahead when Larissa stumbled and slid down a steep hill, coming to a dusty stop at the bottom. Naida saw a big male wolf standing about twenty feet in front of where Larissa was laying. She grabbed her staff and took off running down the hill and was able to get between the wolf and Larissa before it attacked. Her presence changed the wolf's mind about attacking and Larissa was able to get to her feet. Then they both ran, charging the wolf and driving it off before it had time to decide to attack. Hearing all the commotion, Gaea ran back.

"Is everything alright?" Gaea called out, trying to catch her breath.

"Yeah, thanks to Naida." Larissa replied

"It was nothing." Naida said and relayed what had happened to Gaea.

"It could have been worse," Gaea replied, "if you hadn't been there. The wolf would probably have attacked a single person. They find us very easy prey because we're usually slow and awkward."

It was getting close to sunset so the girls decided to go ahead and make camp for the day. They hadn't even made it to the Forbidden Woods, before things got dangerous. They kept watch that night, just in case that wolf brought back friends, but the night went peacefully.

"We should make it to the Forbidden Woods before noon." Gaea said the next morning.

"Sure, if we don't run into any more trouble." Larissa replied.

"Come on," Naida said, "Let's get moving. I'm ready to get this over with. The sooner we start, the sooner we get through."

"What's got you so stirred up?" Gaea asked.

"It's just a feeling." Naida answered. "I feel like we are being watched and I can't shake the feeling. Be extra careful while you're scouting today."

"Yeah, sure," Gaea said, while continuing to look around. "Let's go then."

They set out at a fast pace figuring if someone was following, at least they'd have to do it at a run also. The girls were used to traveling on the run and could keep this up all day. That's why they carried trail jerky to munch on, so they could eat on the run.

Gaea came back, about an hour before dark, to see if they were ready to make camp. There was a good clearing and stream up ahead, which would make a good camp-site.

"Are you ready to stop for the night?" Gaea asked. "I thought we might want to fix a few surprises, in case we have a visitor to-night."

"Good idea," Naida agreed. "We're well into the Forbidden Woods now, no sense in taking chances this early in the game. We'll do the fake camp, for starters."

"Yeah, and a few traps for good measure." Larissa added.

"Sounds good, let's get to it." Gaea agreed.

The girls got busy. A fake camp is when they set up their tents but sleep somewhere else, while still leaving someone on guard. Larissa started the fire while her sisters worked on the traps. The traps were simple snares with trip wires. They would cause trouble for anyone trying to sneak up on them.

The night passed without any intrusions. The girls were actually a little disappointed; they were ready to find out who, or what, had been trailing them. The girls scouted the area while getting firewood that morning. They found wolf tracks.

"It's not possible," Naida said. "A wolf doesn't track anything this far. It can't be the same one."

"The tracks are large enough," Gaea replied. "It's not usual but this may not be a usual wolf. You said, you felt something watching us. It could have been that wolf."

"But why would he be tracking us?" Larissa asked. "That's just creepy."

"Keep a special watch, today," Gaea said. "I'm going to keep a closer watch on our back trail and see what I can see."

"Let me scout today," Naida stated. "I'm better with a bow if there is something out there and your sword is better for close quarters. Besides I've got a surprise for that wolf. I've got some Foxglove I'd like to leave on our back trail; remember what Zona taught us about it?"

"Yeah," Larissa answered. "It's poisonous. If you get it on your skin it can cause a rash."

"That's right," Naida said. "And if you're a wolf and get a good whiff of it you won't be able to smell anything for a while."

"That sounds good," Gaea agreed. "Just be careful."

The girls broke camp and set out at a normal pace, they needed to allow Naida time to circle around and watch their back trail. Gaea led the way, she had a natural sense in the woods, and she had memorized the map Zona gave them. Larissa followed about twenty paces or so behind, enough room to help if needed and far enough back not to get caught in the same trap, if there was one.

They'd traveled for several hours, when Larissa called out for Gaea to hold up. She had seen something down in a gulley and wanted to go and investigate. Gaea came back to see what was going on. As they peered down the hill, they could barely make out a form lying at the bottom.

"It's somebody down there." Larissa said.

"Not somebody," Gaea corrected, "something. That's a troll."

"We need to make sure." Larissa said, dropping her pack.

"No, wait. It may be a trap," Gaea suggested. "Let's wait till Naida comes in, then we can decide what to do. We can't get spread out, just in case."

"What's going on? Naida asked, when she came in a short time later.

"Something's down there," Gaea answered. "And Larissa wants to go down and check it out. I think it's a troll and I'm not sure it's worth it, what do you think?"

"Even if it's a troll, we still have to check it out," Larissa insisted. "It may be hurt."

"Yeah, and it may be a trap," Naida agreed. "But you're right; we do have to check it out. Safety first, though, I'll keep watch while Gaea lets you down with a rope. The wolf is following back there. I couldn't get a shot but I did see it."

Gaea lowered Larissa down the steep slope while Naida kept watch. About half way down, Larissa could tell it was indeed a troll but couldn't tell if it was alive or not. Once on the bottom she looked around, checking for a trap before proceeding to the troll. He was badly hurt, not dead yet but might be soon if they didn't do something.

Larissa fashioned a make-shift stretcher out of some branches and tied the rope to it. She then hollered for Gaea to start pulling, while she brought up the tail end. With Larissa and the stretcher on the rope, Naida had to come over and give Gaea a hand pulling them up. Before they could get them all the way up, the wolf appeared.

Its hackles were up and ready to attack. Gaea tied off the rope, while Naida stood ready to fight. It leaped before Naida could even notch an arrow so she swung the bow. It delivered a good blow to the side of its head, knocking the wolf off to one side, allowing Gaea enough time finish tying it off and come with her sword. As the wolf turned toward Gaea, Naida notched an arrow. The wolf leaped, Gaea was ready and so was Naida. The wolf landed with both the sword and an arrow deep in its flesh… and then it disappeared. The sword and arrow lay on the ground all alone, as if they had been dropped there. The girls looked at each other, looking for confirmation of what had just happened, before rushing back to the rope.

The girls made camp and dressed the troll's wounds, which were serious but not fatal. While he was resting, the girls finally had a chance to talk.

"We did see that, didn't we?" Naida asked.

"Yeah, we saw it. The darkness makes cold chills run up my spine and Broom-rider has to be behind it. She has been after us for a long time and now has sent this wolf by magic somehow," Gaea responded. "She has to be involved in all this, but why?"

"She hates everything about the Rings and the people who wear them," Larissa suggested. "What more of a reason would she need?"

"Yeah, we are going to settle that debt one day," Naida agreed. "Now, what are we going to do with this troll?"

"Let's see how he is in the morning," Larissa said. "Then we can decide."

The next morning, the troll was better but still not speaking to them. Since he was unable to travel, the girls fixed him a shelter and left him enough food and water for a few days. They had to send Larissa back down the hill to get his weapons, which they left within his reach as they were leaving.

It was going to be at least two more days before they made it out of the Forbidden Woods. They traveled that day without incident, which they were thankful for. There had been way too much excitement this trip. Tomorrow should see them out.

The following day started beautifully. It was a perfect day. The sun was shining, the birds were singing, and the trolls attacked about noon. The girls were able to make it to some rocks, close to a ravine. They could hold the trolls off for days here.

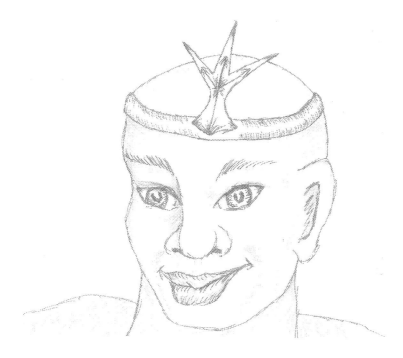

"You need to take Larissa and head down the ravine," Gaea said. "You'll be able to make it out of here. It's only another half a day travel, to get out of the forest."

"And what happens to you?" Naida asked. "What do you plan to do?"

"I can hold them off and give you plenty of time to get away, but if we all leave, then they'll follow," Gaea said. "I'm the oldest, so it's my choice. Now go, before it's too late."

Naida and Larissa made it down to the ravine without the trolls knowing that they had left. The ravine ran north, which was the way they needed to head. They traveled for about two hours, enough time to be well away from the trolls. Then they started to back track, slowly making their way back to the place where the trolls attacked. Shortly before dark they reached the place and no one was around. The trolls and Gaea were both gone.

Larissa and Naida searched the area, looking for sign and could tell by the tracks that the trolls had captured Gaea. They couldn't tell if she was alive but there was no blood. The girls followed the tracks to a small village near by. From their vantage point, they could see their sister in a cage, in the center of the huts. She seemed to be alright…so far. They weren't sure what trolls did with prisoners and weren't planning on finding out. As soon as it was dark, they were going to sneak in and get her out.

The trolls must feel safe; they didn't even set a guard. Naida and Larissa separated and came into the village from two different directions. Hoping if one was discovered, then the other one could release Gaea. Both girls made it to Gaea's cage without incident. This was going to be too easy. Too late, they noticed the trap. That's why there was no guard, Gaea was bait and they fell into the trap. A net fell over the girls trapping them and before they could get out, they were surrounded by trolls.

"Hey sis, we're here to rescue you." Naida said as the trolls threw them in the cage.

"And doing a great job too," Gaea replied. Sometimes humor is all you have.

"How did they get you? Larissa asked, as she picked herself off the ground.

"Blow dart," Gaea answered. "You left just in time; they got up above me before I realized it. That juice they use sure packs a wallop, I was out in seconds."

"Do you know what they do with prisoners?" Larissa asked.

"Make us slaves, I think, if we cooperate," Gaea answered. "We may as well get some sleep. Tomorrow could be very interesting."

The next morning the girls were brought, bound, before the chief. "My name is Shermac, I am chief of this village; what were you doing in our forest?"

"We were just passing through," Gaea answered, standing tall and looking him straight in the eyes. "Why were we attacked?"

"There is a reason these woods are called Forbidden," the chief replied. "This is our territory and we do not appreciate intruders."

Before the girls could answer, the troll that they had helped came limping into the village. The girls were put back in the cage, while the trolls gathered around him. There was a lot of talking and arm waving. Eventually, the girls were brought back before Shermac.

The chief began. "My son tells me that you helped him earlier. Why did you do that?"

"Because he needed it," Naida stated, matter-of-factly. "We never leave an injured person to die if we can help. Our father and grand-mother taught us better than that."

"Yes, I saw the sword… and the red hair," the chief puzzled. "Do you know Beltar?"

"Yes, he's our father, or was," Gaea answered. "How do you know him?"

"We call him friend," Shermac replied. "He has helped us many times in our dealings with humans. You said was?"

"He was killed by two dragons, in the Shaderack Mountains, three years ago," Gaea said. "We've been with our grand-mother, Zona, since then. She is the one who sent us on this trip."

"Yes, we know Zona as well. This is my son, Hans," the chief said, indicating the injured troll. "Please except our apology for any inconvenience. You are free to go, and I hope that we may call you friends also."

"To call you friend would be our honor, Chief Shermac." Gaea responded with a nod and bow.

"Yes, you are very much like your father." Shermac said as he waved good-bye, thinking of the last time he saw Beltar a year ago.

When the girls returned to Truitt, Zona was waiting at the edge of the village and came running to greet them. She was so relieved to see them back, safe and sound. After hearing their story, she was pleased that they had made friends with Shermac and worried about the wolf. Broom-rider would be dealt with soon enough and hopefully end this reign of darkness.

"Well, after all this adventure," Zona began. "What have you learned about love?"

"I've learned that you will do whatever it takes to protect someone you care about, even if it puts you in danger," Naida said.

"Yeah, and you will help anyone in need, even if they're supposed to be an enemy," Larissa added.

"I learned that you will sacrifice yourself to benefit the ones you love," Gaea finished. "There is no price too high to save them."

"Very good," Zona said smiling. "I couldn't have said it better myself. Love means sacrifice. Love never requires or demands, love always gives. The Ring of Love is my favorite ring of all. This will be the best celebration ever."

As the girls were heading up-stairs for a long needed rest, Gaea asked Naida what about her boy-friend. "He's a jerk," Naida said and they all laughed. They were thinking that love may not be easy but it was worth it.

CHAPTER 8
RESPONSIBILITY

Zona and the girls were talking about their studies when Larissa asked, "Grand-ma? What's the difference between being steadfast and being stubborn?"

"That's really a very good question," Zona replied. "It depends on your point of view I guess. For instance if I agree with you then I would say you are being steadfast. If I disagreed with you then you'd be stubborn."

"That's not fair," Naida replied. "It shouldn't depend on what someone else thinks. It's either one or the other."

"Very good," Zona agreed. "I was wondering if you were going to let me get away with that. It does depend on your point of view though, because your view is what you're going to judge what another person does."

"Ok, let's try it this way," Zona continued. "If you were hanging from a rope and the fall would be a thousand feet, then for you to keep hanging on would be steadfast. Now if the fall would only be one foot, then to keep hanging on would be stubborn."

"I think I understand," Gaea said slowly. "It really depends on the consequences of you changing your mind."

"Yeah," Larissa interrupted. "The more severe the consequences then the more steadfast you should be."

"You know our mother fell from a rope, don't you?" Naida asked.

"Yes, but that's not the same thing," Zona said very firmly. "Not the same thing at all. Your mother gave her life so that you wouldn't lose both your father and mother in that accident. Your mother did what she had to do and I hope you can see the difference."

"Yes, grand-ma," Naida replied. "But we still miss her…well… them, very much."

"I know dear, so do I," Zona said. "And on that cheery note I must be off. I've got to get on the road before it gets any later. Carmen will think I've changed my mind about coming. Are you sure that you girls will be ok while I'm gone?"

"Yes, we'll be fine," Gaea said. "You just go and take care of your sick friend."

"I sorry I'm going to miss your birthday, Larissa." Zona said as she was walking out the door.

"I know," Larissa yelled back to her. "I understand and have a safe trip and try to have some fun, we'll be fine."

Larissa's birthday was just a few days away and Gaea and Naida wanted to get her something really special since Zona was going to miss it and they were all missing their parents. They figured if they could find a special present then it would cheer her up. Gaea had gotten her a pair of ear-rings like a pair of hers that she liked so much, Naida got her a walking stick made by the elves, and Zona had made her a new dress before she left but they really wanted something special.

Gaea and Naida were hunting north of Truitt, close to the mountains, when they found a rock. This wasn't just any rock; it was perfectly round and as smooth as glass. It was about the size of a basketball and looked like it would be heavy but it wasn't. It was extremely light. This would make a perfect present for Larissa because it was definitely one of a kind and they knew she would love it.

The day of her birthday finally came. The girls had gone on a picnic that day and fixed a huge supper that night. When it was time for presents they gathered in the den in front of the fireplace since the nights were still a bit cool. First Gaea gave her the ear-rings, then Naida gave her the walking stick, and they both gave her the dress from Zona. She was really pleased with the gifts and thanked her sisters for their time and effort on her birthday but it just wasn't the same without Zona. That's when they brought out the rock. She was so surprised, she started crying. Not just that the rock was so amazing but that they had gone to the extra effort, just for her. This rock made today a very special day.

The girls decided to call it a night, banked the fire and headed upstairs to bed. Larissa remembered that she had left the rock on the fireplace. She decided it would be alright until morning; it had been a long and happy day.

The girls were awoken by a sharp cracking sound coming from downstairs. They all came running out of their rooms with weapons in hand. Gaea had her sword, Naida a club, and Larissa had her new walking stick.

"What was that?" Larissa asked

"I don't know," Gaea answered. "It sounded like something breaking."

"Well, go see what it was," Naida suggested.

"Not me," Larissa said. "Gaea, you go see."

"We'll all go," Gaea said, with more confidence than she felt.

As the girls made it downstairs, they heard it again. It was coming from the den. The girls made it to the door just in time to see the rock fall off the fireplace and land on the floor. It hit hard and continued to roll around in circles. They saw a crack starting to show in the rock.

"No," Larissa cried, "As she ran to grab her rock." She just knew it was broken now.

But before she could get to the rock, out popped a small dragon head. Larissa stopped so quickly that Naida and Gaea ran into her, before they could stop. The girls stared as the dragon slowly pecked and twisted its way out of the rock, egg. Finally free, the dragon wobbled and squawked all around the room, until Larissa finally picked it up.

The dragon was friendly and liked to be held but it wasn't exactly cuddly. The scales were soft and flexible but they were still kind of scratchy. It didn't seem dangerous; after all it was just a baby. That's what she would call it, Baby. It was a baby and they didn't know if it was male or female so that would fit either way. The girls made it a bed in an old wooden box and went back to bed. They'd decide what to do in the morning.

When the girls came down the next morning, they found the dragon curled up in the ashes of the fireplace. The girls fixed breakfast and the dragon ate eggs, bacon, and biscuits but of course it wasn't cooked. After eating, the girls were playing with Baby in the den. Gaea was pulling a string and Baby was chasing it. It turns out that dragons are more curious than a cat and a lot more playful. The dragon all of a sudden got the hic-ups. The first time it hic-upped it burnt up Zona's favorite chair, the second time, the coffee table, and before they could get Baby into the fireplace they also lost the couch.

It seems that when baby dragons get the hic-ups, they blow fire, not just any fire, dragon-fire. Dragon-fire instantly consumes whatever it touches.

"What are we going to do now?" Larissa asked.

"We?" the girls said together, "That's your dragon."

"Seriously," Larissa pleaded. "We've got to replace all this stuff before Zona gets back."

"Okay, okay." Gaea said. "Don't worry, we'll think of something."

It turns out that dragons are very good at catching mice. Larissa took Baby around the village and hired him out as a mouser. Baby cleared all mice out of the grain storage in just a few days. He also cleared a few houses around Truitt. Gaea and Naida helped by cleaning houses or chopping wood, anything they could do to make some money.

By the time that Zona returned to Truitt, the girls had more than enough money to replace the furniture. When she had heard the whole story, Zona was pleased by the girl's actions, but she wanted to know what they were going to do now.

"What do you intend to do with Baby now?" Zona asked.

"We've been thinking about that," Gaea answered. "We found the egg at the bottom of the mountain, so its mother must be somewhere around."

"That's a Rock Dragon," Zona said. "The mother doesn't take care of the young; they can take care of themselves from birth. There should be other babies in the area though."

"Then that's what we'll do," Larissa said. "We'll take Baby back and find his friends."

Zona was able to tell them that the dragon was a boy but they still called him Baby. The girls packed a few supplies because they weren't sure how long this would take, and they didn't want to leave him without knowing that he would be able to take care of himself. Zona agreed that he may be too tame to be freed right away.

The girls left early the next morning, and they made a funny caravan. The girls loaded down with their packs and a baby dragon following after, flapping its wings and squawking behind them. It took all day to make it to the top of the mountain so the girls decided to set up camp next to a stream and find the other dragons tomorrow.

Baby was constantly underfoot as Naida was trying to fix supper. Baby was good help getting the fire started but every time Naida took out any food to fix Baby would eat it. Naida finally sent Baby over to Gaea, who was setting up the tents. Every time Gaea would tie off the rope to a stake and go to the next one Baby would untie it and the tent would keep falling down. Gaea sent Baby over to help Larissa, who was getting the sleeping bags out. Larissa would stretch out a bag and Baby would grab it and start a tug-of -war with it. Larissa found herself chasing Baby down just to get the sleeping bag back. Finally, she closed Baby up in one until everybody got finished with what they were doing. When everything was ready, they let Baby out while they ate. It had been a long, hard day so they all decided to turn in early.

The next morning, the girls set out to find some other dragons. They found some tracks a little further down the stream, and followed them into a meadow. There in the middle of the clearing was maybe half a dozen babies playing. Baby heard their squawking and took off running, well; it was more like a waddle, right into the middle of the group. The other babies gathered around him squawking back and forth. He seemed to have been accepted.

The girls watched the dragons from the top of a hill. They were all different colors. Baby was red and gold, the others were green and orange, or blue and silver, all the colors of the rainbow were present. It was a beautiful sight to sit and watch the multitude of colors shifting and swaying in the tall meadow grass as the dragons hopped and jumped over and around each other. After a few hours, the girls decided to leave them on their own, and headed back to camp.

The next day, the girls found the dragons in the same clearing, but today they were playing on a small hill at the edge of the mountain. The dragons would take off running and flapping their wings, and then launch themselves off the hill, only to glide down to the bottom. Baby was in the midst of them although he wasn't doing quite as well as the others. Evidently, he was a little behind in his training because of being with the girls.

"I hope he'll be able to keep up with the others," Larissa said.

"He'll be fine," Naida replied. "It may take him a little while, but he'll catch up in no time."

"Yeah," Gaea continued. "After all, he got a little of the woodlands in him. He'll be fine."

As the day progressed, Baby did improve. It was fun to watch him take off and soar down to the ground. His gliding was getting better and better, but his landings were hilarious. He would hit with his feet stretched out but he would hit, bounce and roll. The other dragons weren't much better; the girls would burst out laughing every time one would land. The dragons, evidently could hear their laughter because they would look their way when they got a little too loud. The girls decided to leave them alone for their flight training; besides their sides were hurting from all the laughter.

"I'm so glad that he seems to be doing so good." Larissa said. "It's just like he's my own kid. I worry about him when he's not around."

"I guess that's normal," Gaea replied. "But you will still have to leave him out here, sooner or later."

"I know, but I'm still very proud of how well he's doing." Larissa said, while dreaming of the time he'll be soaring high up in the sky.

"Well, I'm going to see if I can get some fresh meat," Naida said. "It's starting to get too sentimental around here."

"Hey!" Larissa exclaimed.

"Wait for me," Gaea said, holding back the laughter. "I'll go with you."

The girls had fresh rabbit that night for supper, and then turned in early, looking forward to tomorrow. They wouldn't let Larissa know it but they were proud of Baby too.

Not long after going to sleep, the girls awoke to a rumbling in the bushes. This area was considered safe so they hadn't bothered with keeping a guard but their senses were attuned to strange sounds, and this was definitely strange. Rule #47… Never look into the campfire at night; you won't be able to see your surroundings.

All of a sudden the sound was all around them, and it was coming closer. The girls were on their feet with weapons in hand, ready for an attack. They stood in the center with their backs to each other, facing outward. The rustling got louder and louder until finally they could see shapes come bursting out of the woods. It was the dragons and they were coming full force with Baby in the lead. Evidently, they were seeking revenge for the girls laughing at them earlier.

The girls tried to chase them off but the dragons thought it was a game. While they chased some away from their tents, others were scattering their supplies. When they went after those, some others would drag their sleeping bags away. It was a never ending deal and the girls didn't have a chance. Finally, the girls gave up and collapsed in a heap. Looking around, the camp was a shambles. The tents were lying on the ground, their supplies were scattered everywhere, and the sleeping bags were somehow up in a tree. *Can dragons climb trees?*

Seeing the surrender, the dragons stopped the escapades and followed Baby toward the girls. While Baby curled up in Larissa's lap, Naida and Gaea straightened the camp. Luckily, the dragons brought the sleeping bags back, and yes dragons can climb trees, baby dragons anyway (a good thing to know for future reference). After modest repairs to the camp, they all laid down to rest. Baby was still with Larissa and the others were scattered around Gaea and Naida. It was kind of nice, having them around, Naida thought before falling asleep.

The next morning, the dragons were gone when the girls awoke. The girls finished straightening the camp, ate breakfast, and went to find the dragons again in the same field, practicing take-offs and landings. It was going to be a while before any of them mastered it. The girls were very careful to keep the laughter to themselves.

Over the next few weeks, the dragons got better and better until they were actually flying. The take-offs were shaky but the landings were hilarious. They would come in, feet extended, in what would look like a perfect landing, and then they would hit, bounce, and start rolling and bouncing to a screeching halt. In spite of the girl's best efforts, they could not keep from rolling with laughter. The dragons watched the girls closely but it seemed that they were also doing some laughing of their own.

Finally, the dragons got it down to perfection. They would come flying in, feet extended and then at just the right moment, flair their wings to slow their speed and drop to the ground with a soft thud. The girls would applaud just as loud as they had laughed. It was a beautiful sight to behold.

The girls decided it was time to say good-by. As they came walking down the hill to the meadow, it seems that Baby knew what was about to happen. He came to meet them and the others were right behind him. Remembering that dragons communicate with mental pictures Larissa saw a picture of the dragons flying away. Yes, she nodded and sent a picture of her and her sisters leaving also.

The girls had to swallow a lump in their throats, as they watched the dragons all take flight; they circled once, and then headed west into the sunset.

"I am really going to miss them," Larissa said, choking back the tears.

"Me too," Naida agreed.

"Well, it's about time we got back to the real world anyway," Gaea said, sounding just a little bit too gruff as she turned and walked away. She couldn't let her sisters see the tears in her eyes. "Let's get packed up, so we can leave first thing in the morning."

The return trip was uneventful, and maybe even a little boring. The girls walked in silence all the way back to Truitt. Zona met them at the door as they came in and asked how it went. The girls told all about the dragons and the events of the past several weeks.

"Well, I must admit, that I am very proud of you three," Zona said. "You have proven that you are ready for your next ring, the Ring of Responsibility. You took it upon yourselves to replace the things that Baby destroyed, and did not shirk from doing what was right for him."

"I didn't want to let him go, though." Larissa said blankly.

"That's what I'm talking about," Zona continued. "Even when you wanted him to stay, you still let him go, because that was best for him. That's taking responsibility."

"Well," Naida said, "I'm not sure I like being responsible, but I do enjoy getting another ring."

"Yeah," Gaea added, "and another party too."

The girls received their rings at the next full moon. The celebration lasted long into the night, and the girls had something to remember Baby by… something besides ashes. The girls could not help but wonder where Baby was now and what was he doing and if they would ever see him again. Some of the rings were fun to earn, some were dangerous, and some were sad, but all were necessary. Just a few more to earn and they would be ready to face the darkness and Broom-rider would finally get what was coming to her.

CHAPTER 9
PATIENCE

As this story opens up we find the Woodland girls in one of their training sessions with Zona. This particular session was dealing with patience. The topic came up because the girls were worrying too much about things that couldn't be helped. This was their third lesson on patience but it just wasn't sinking in. Gaea was about grown and she felt like she should be able to make her own decisions and have her own place. That way she could have a real life. Naida was getting older but she felt like everyone was still treating her like a child. Larissa wanted everything "NOW". Zona was getting tired of hearing "I just can't wait" so she decided to try something else.

"I just can't wait until my birthday," Naida said, for the umpteenth time. "I'll finally be sixteen and the party is going to be huge. All my friends will be there."

"Yeah, well I can't wait until I can move out and get my own place," Gaea replied. "That's when you're really grown up."

Zona came in just as this was going on. "I think you're both right. You seem to have a problem learning patience so I'm going to try something else. I'm going to grant each of you one wish."

"Do I get a wish too?" Larissa asked.

"Of course," Zona replied. "You need to think before you decide what your wish is."

"I don't need to think about it," Gaea replied quickly. "I know exactly what I want. I want my own place. That's what I wish for."

"If you're sure that's what you want, I'll see what I can do." Zona said.

"I know what I want too," Naida said. "I want to have my party now, if I can. I don't want to wait another couple of weeks."

Zona replied. "That I know we can do. How does tonight sound? You can tell all your friends and I can get everything ready."

"That will be perfect!" Naida said, running out the door. "I'm going to tell them all now."

"What about you Larissa?" Zona asked. "Do you know what you want now?"

"No, I don't know yet. Is it ok if I think on it a while?" Larissa requested.

"Sure that will be fine." Zona answered. "Now, Gaea, do you mind helping me with the party? Then we can see about finding your own place."

"Oh yeah, that will be fine. I'm so excited; this is going to be great! Finally my own place," Gaea said. "Now I've got to get busy on Naida's birthday gift."

Zona went into the kitchen to get started on baking Naida's cake. Double-chocolate with chocolate icing was her favorite. Larissa followed because she loved helping in the kitchen. She always got to lick the spoon. Gaea came in a little while later to help out. In no time at all everything was ready.

Naida came back with most of her friends in tow. Her best-friend was gone with her mother to visit family in the next village and Bobby, the guy she kind of liked, was out on a hunting trip but everybody else was there. There was singing and music. Zona and her sisters had prepared a feast. This party was going to be the talk of the village.

Naida got plenty of presents too: Gaea gave her traveling shoes made by elves, Larissa had made her enough arrows to fill a quiver and they were very well done too, and Zona of course gave her a beautiful dress. Her friends gave her things like jewelry, a scarf, some gloves and a knife she had been wanting. It was past mid-night when Naida said good-night to the last of the guests. She was worn out as she headed up-stairs to bed.

"That was the best birthday ever," Naida told Zona, as she gave her a hug good-night. "Thank you so much for letting me have my party now. It was everything I'd hoped it would be."

"You're welcome, child." She replied. "I'm so glad you enjoyed it. I'll see you in the morning."

The next morning, Zona came in just as the girls were finishing breakfast. "I've found you a place, Gaea. The Morgan's old cottage is empty and the elders said you could move right in. It just needs a good cleaning."

"That is great, grandma," Gaea exclaimed. "Come on Naida, let's go and have a look."

They took off out the door, with Larissa following, "Hey, wait for me."

The girls worked all that day cleaning, dusting, washing, and wiping down the entire cottage. Zona brought over some curtains for the windows and some extra dishes for Gaea to use. Naida promised to help Gaea move her bed and a few pieces of furniture tomorrow. On the way back to Zona's that night Gaea stopped by the inn to talk to Zelda. She was hoping that Zelda would need help around the inn because if she was going to be on her own, she was going to need a job.

Zelda was more than happy to hire Gaea as there was always something that needed doing and she knew how good a worker Gaea was. The girls had been a big help back when Princess Sara had come to Truitt. Everything was working out beautifully. She had a place of her own and a job. What more could a person want?

Early the next day, Gaea and Naida were moving the rest of Gaea's things. She had to get finished today because tomorrow she was going to start working at the inn. They worked hard all that day and finished up early that evening. Gaea decided that she would fix supper for Naida, to thank her for all her help.

"Isn't this great?" Gaea asked Naida, while they were sitting around after eating. "I've got my own place. No matter how many times I say it, it still doesn't seem real."

"Yeah, it is nice," Naida agreed. "You can just sit around and not have to worry about anybody or anything."

"Yep, my own place," Gaea repeated, musing about how good life was going to be now.

The following days found Gaea working all day at the inn, only to come home and fix supper, wash some clothes, straighten the house, and go to bed so she could start all over again tomorrow. It didn't take her too long to start wondering if this is all life is about; work, eat, and sleep.

She started thinking about the way it was at Zona's and realized that it really didn't matter where you were, what mattered the most is who you're with. Family is the most important thing in life. To win a card game by yourself was no fun, without someone else to share it with or walking in the woods and noticing a beautiful sunset without someone else to see it took the value out of it. Gaea was starting to regret her decision to move out.

She was invited back to Zona's on Naida's real birthday, which was only a couple of days away, to eat supper. There wouldn't be a party or anything but she was really looking forward to going and being with all of them. It was no fun at all to eat every meal by yourself.

Finally the day arrived and Gaea went straight there from the inn. She was anxious to see them again, even her baby sister Larissa. When she arrived, Naida and Larissa were playing a card game and arguing. She couldn't believe how loud it was, she had gotten used to the quiet of an empty house. Boy, did it sound good. They both looked up when she entered, and said hi, not bothering to stop the argument for a second to give a hug. That's silly she thought to herself, *I never cared about hugging them before.* Zona was in the kitchen finishing supper. Gaea struck her head in to see if she could help.

"My Goodness, no," Zona exclaimed. "You are our guest. You march right in there and have a seat; supper will be ready in no time."

"Yes, ma'am," Gaea said, a little disappointed. "If you're sure you don't need any help?"

She left with Zona rustling around in the kitchen, humming a tune. She took a seat in the den and was watching her sisters play their game. When it finally ended, she let herself get talked into playing the next one. This is what makes life worth living, Gaea thought to herself.

Zona came in and was watching the girls, not wanting to interrupt their game to tell them that supper was ready, it was good to have Gaea back home. After eating, everybody pitched in to clean the dishes and the kitchen. Zona agreed to play a game or two with the girls. While they were playing, Gaea broached the subject.

"Do you think I might be able to move back in? It's not that I can't make it, because I can. It's just that I don't want to, at least, not yet. I never realized how much all this really meant to me, family I mean, doing things together even if it's just a card game. I miss all of this and I really do want to come back home." Gaea eyes were a bit wet in spite of her best efforts.

"Of course, you can come back. That's exactly what I was hoping for. It hasn't been the same around here either. Your sisters only had each other to fight and argue with. This is and always will be, your home," Zona said.

Zona called all the girls to gather around. "Well girls, I guess you heard what Gaea was saying. Now I would like to ask what you now know about patience."

Gaea started. "I've learned that it's not just waiting on something special, it's enjoying each day as you wait."

"Yeah" Naida agreed. "I've learned that the enjoyment and anticipation of looking forward to something is half the fun. Today is my birthday but it's not that special now, it's the party and celebration that makes it special. My rushing it meant my best friend and the boy I liked couldn't come and be apart of it."

"Very good," Zona replied. "Well now, Larissa, what about you? Have you decided what you want for your wish?"

"Well…I think I'd like some pizza," Larissa said.

"Are you sure that's what you want? You just ate a few hours ago," Zona asked.

"Yes ma'am, that's what I want and I want it now," Larissa affirmed, with her hands on her hips.

"Okay," Zona said, heading into the kitchen. She returned in a few moments with a frozen pizza.

"But it's not cooked," Larissa pouted.

"I know," Zona agreed. "You said you wanted it, now."

"Well, I guess I've learned something too," Larissa said. "If something is worth having, then it's worth waiting for."

"That's exactly right," Zona agreed. "That's the most important lesson of all."

Zona and the girls played games long into the night and even had pizza later when it was cooked. They talked of finally having the Ring of Patience but no one had a problem of waiting until the next full moon. There were only a few more rings to earn and the girls would probably get a little impatient before it was over with.

CHAPTER 10
FRIENDSHIP

The story of this ring opens with Zona and the girls cleaning the house and getting ready for company. There were some visitors coming to Truitt from another village and Zona was going to let them stay here for a while. Gaea had been working hard, cleaning up and doing a lot of cooking but she still wasn't very happy about having to do all this extra work for a bunch of strangers.

"I still don't see why they have to stay here," Gaea complained.

Zona replied, "They're strangers to this area and they need our help, besides it's the friendly thing to do."

"Yeah," Larissa said. "Don't you remember our lessons of friendship?"

"I'm glad you agree, Larissa, but that's not exactly right," Zona corrected. "We're acting friendly but they aren't our friends, at least not yet. We don't know them well enough to be friends. Remember that friends are the most important people in the world."

"What about family?" Naida asked.

"Family is important, don't get me wrong but you don't pick your family," Zona said, continuing with the lesson. "I know that sounds strong but think about it. Who do you spend most of your time with? Who is it that shares your tears and joys? Who influences everything you think, say, or do?"

"I know," Larissa said, "Your friends."

"That's right," Zona agreed. "So remember how important the decision is before you make friends with the wrong person."

"How can you know if a person is going to be a good friend or not before you make friends with them?" Gaea asked.

"Well, I guess, when you know that, you'll have your next ring?" Zona said, smiling.

Before Zona could continue with the lesson their guests arrived. As it turns out this family had two children, a girl about Naida's age, Tina, and a boy just a year older than Gaea, Tony. All of a sudden, Gaea was willing to help anyway she could and I'm sure it had nothing to do with the way Tony looked. He was quite handsome and very cool, according to Naida.

Gaea was just coming back downstairs, after carrying their bags to the rooms, when her best friend, Terri, arrived. Gaea was going to spend the night with Terri because Zona needed her room for the guests. Gaea and Terri had been friends for a long time and she was looking forward to spending some time with her.

Zona answered the door. "Well, hello Terri. It's good to see you again. May I introduce you to our guests? This is Mr. and Mrs. Farmer. That young lady over there is their daughter, Tina, and the fellow is their son, Tony."

"Hello, it's nice to meet you," Terri began, until she got a good look at Tony, then she began to stutter. "Hi, uh, so, uh, your name is, uh, Tony."

"Yes it is," Tony said, coming over to shake her hand.

Gaea just knew there was going to be trouble; they both looked like love-sick puppies. "Well, we need to be going, Terri… Terri? Are you ready to go?"

Finally Gaea was able to drag Terri out the door. All the way to Terri's house it was Tony this and Tony that. Gaea thought that Tony was cool and good-looking too, but why did Terri have all the luck? In the time it took to walk to Terri's house, she must have heard Tony's name a thousand times. Do you think he likes me? Isn't he just a dream? We need to go back there tomorrow. On, and on, and on. Why couldn't she just hush about Tony and talk about something else.

Mean while, back at Zona's, Naida and Larissa had taken Tina upstairs to their room to play. Tina didn't want to play any of the games the girls suggested. They were childish or her other favorite saying was, "that's just dumb". Finally, Tina led the girls back downstairs and they slipped out the door. When they reached the trees, Tina pulled out some tobacco and rolled a cigarette. After taking a couple of puffs she asked the girls if they wanted some.

"No," Naida and Larissa said in unison. "We don't smoke."

"Why?" Tina asked. "Are you scared? If you're not scared then you'd smoke."

"We're not scared," Naida said, starting to get aggravated. "We don't smoke because we don't want to. Smoking is bad for you."

"Ah, you're just a fraidy cat," Tina taunted. "I've been smoking for years and it hasn't hurt me."

"No we're not, besides we need to get back before Zona finds out we're gone," Larissa said.

"Afraid to smoke and afraid of the dark too," Tina snickered. "I can tell this is going to be a fun week."

The Farmer's were planning on staying in Truitt for about a week or until they could find a place of their own. The girls weren't sure they'd make it; Tina was a pain in the neck. The next morning Naida and Larissa took Tina around to show her the town. All they heard from Tina was, her town was a lot better, they had a bigger church, and their inn was a lot nicer. After a day of this, they were fit to be tied. They took Tina back to Zona's and went to find Gaea. She was at Terri's but Terri was gone off with Tony. The girls decided that tomorrow they would go on a picnic, just the three of them. It would be good to get away for awhile.

The girls okayed it with Zona and left early in the morning to go to their favorite spot by the river. It was a beautiful day and the girls were having a wonderful time. After eating lunch, they were sitting around talking.

"I believe I'll scream if I hear the name Tony one more time," Gaea said. "That's all she talks about. They have so much in common; even their names start with the same letter. I'm sick of hearing how cool he is."

Naida asked, "Don't you think you're acting a little bit jealous? After all, before he picked Terri, you thought he was pretty cool too."

"Yeah, maybe I did," Gaea agreed. "But that was when I thought he had better taste in girls."

They all laughed because they knew Gaea was joking. Then she continued, "I guess I can't blame Terri. He is good-looking, besides Terri and I have been friends for a long time. She's my best friend and we've been through a lot together. That's enough about me, how are you and Tina getting along?"

"You've got to be kidding," Naida said. "She's a real pain in the neck. Nothing we do is ever good enough for her. Her house is better than Zona's, her village is better than Truitt, and she's always trying to talk us into something. Did you know that she smokes?"

"Well, have you told Zona how she is?" Gaea asked.

"No, it wouldn't do any good," Naida said. "She wouldn't make them leave; besides it won't be too much longer now, even if it does seem like forever."

The girls packed up and headed back to Truitt; they promised to be back before dark. The next few days seemed to drag by. Naida and Larissa continued trying to be nice to Tina but she was never satisfied. The bed was too soft, the room was too hot, or the food wasn't very good. Now everybody knows that Zona is the best cook in the country. That proves there is no pleasing her but they continued to try.

Gaea had decided to try a little harder too. She helped Terri get ready for her date by fixing her hair up and even let Terri wear her favorite necklace. She had to admit Tony and Terri made a good couple. The next few days passed without any major concerns until the time finally came for the Farmers to be leaving in the morning.

Gaea and her sisters were helping Zona fix a big going away party for the Farmers. Gaea even invited Terri to come over for supper. The evening went surprisingly well; even Tina seemed to be in a better mood. They all sat around talking and laughing and were having a good time. It was a good finish to a very long visit.

The next morning the Farmers were on their way and the girls were glad it was over with and things could get back to normal again. Zona called the girls into the den to see if they'd learned anything by the Farmer's visit.

"Well girls, now that the Farmers are gone, what do you now know about friendship?" Zona asked.

Gaea started. "Well, I believe I have learned a lot. I was a bit jealous at first when Tony picked Terri instead of me. Then I decided that Terri and I have been friends a long time and I wasn't going to lose that friendship over a guy I just met."

"Very good," Zona said. "Now, how about you two?"

"I really tried to be friends with Tina but it just didn't work," Naida replied.

"Me too," Larissa added. "No matter what we did, it was never good enough."

"Well it looks like you've all learned a lot about friendship. A new friend should never take the place of an old one. And girls, not everyone that you act friendly toward, will become your friend. Especially, if they're as big a pain as Tina was," Zona said, smiling.

"You mean you knew how she was acting?" Larissa asked.

"Of course," Zona replied. "That's the main reason you've earned the Ring of Friendship. To be friendly toward someone that isn't being very nice is the hardest test of friendship."

It was just a week away from the full moon, when they could get their rings. The girls decided that they should invite the Farmers to the celebration.

CHAPTER 11
HAPPINESS

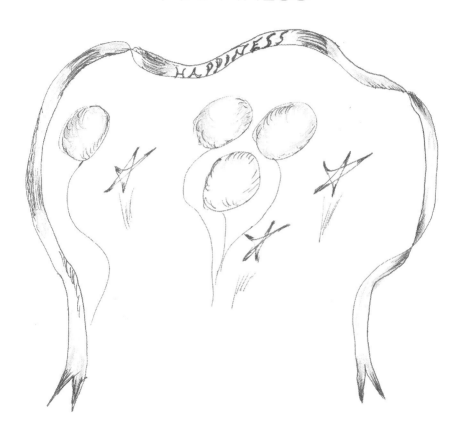

We find the Woodland girls in yet another lesson with Zona, just one of many since the girls started working on their Rings of Power. This ring, if they're able to earn it, will be their last: the Ring of Happiness.

Zona explains. "Because happiness is often so hard to obtain, many ring bearers only have nine. You can still be a Ring Master with nine, that's a decision each of you will have to decide. This ring is so difficult to earn it is always last, even to the ones that do eventually earn it, so don't feel bad if it eludes you too."

"Do you have the Ring of Happiness? Larissa asked.

"Yes, and it was the last one for me too," Zona replied. "Now to give you a chance to learn this lesson, I'm going to grant each of you one wish. Give it plenty of thought, what is the one thing that would make you happy?"

As the girls left that day, they were talking about all the things that would make them happy. Zona just shook her head, she wasn't sure if they would be able to earn this ring or not. Very few people ever learned true happiness, that's why most ring bearers only wore nine. Happiness is so hard to find and even harder to keep. Well, it's up to the girls now.

The girls thought for several days on what to wish for. They would think of something and then reject it, think of something else and then reject that too. Finally, Naida and Gaea thought they were ready. They found Zona with Larissa in the kitchen.

"I know what I want with my wish, grandma." Naida said.

"That's great," Zona replied. "You finally know what it will take to make you happy?"

"Yes, I thought on it long and hard and finally made up my mind," Naida said, proudly. "I first thought of money but there are so many things that money can't buy, like an Elfin Hunters' Jacket. That's what I want. I don't think I'll ever be able to earn it so this may be the only chance I have to ever get one. You can't buy one so if you can get me one I'd be happy."

"Okay, that's quite a request but if you're sure that's what you want,"

Zona replied. "I'll talk to Chanook, the Elf Prince, and see if he'll get you one. Now, have you decided Gaea?"

"Yeah, I've decided too," Gaea said. "I'd give anything for a date with this certain boy, he's so cute, but he doesn't even know that I exist. He's name is David and his family just moved to Truitt. Do you really think you can get me a date with him? If I could go on a date with David, I know he would like me too."

"I believe so, if that's what you really want to be happy?" Zona answered.

"Yes, yes, yes. That's what I really want," Gaea replied, jumping up and down.

"And Larissa have you decided?" Zona asked.

"I think so," Larissa said slowly. "I've had a hard time deciding because I have everything I need, but watching you cook gave me an idea. I have never had a five layer German chocolate cake with vanilla icing all to myself."

"Are you crazy?" Naida and Gaea said in unison.

Even Zona was surprised. "That has got to be the strangest request I've ever heard, but if that's what you want, then that's what you'll get, I'll bake it today."

Zona continued. "Very well, if you're all sure that these requests are what you really want, then so be it. I hope that they will bring you the happiness that you seek."

The girls all nodded their heads in agreement and left Zona baking the cake for Larissa. That night after supper, she brought out the cake and set it before Larissa. After eating three pieces, herself, she offered some to her sisters.

"No, Larissa," Zona responded. "That cake is just for you."

"I don't have to eat it all, tonight, do I?" Larissa pleaded.

"Oh no, you can do whatever you want with it, whatever makes you happy," Zona said.

"Then I'd like to share it. It is so delicious, I want all of you to enjoy it too," Larissa replied.

'Very well," Zona agreed. "If you're sure that's what you want. I'd love a piece."

"Me too," Gaea and Naida said, fighting to be the next in line, as Larissa cut each of them a piece.

The next morning Naida went to the elf camp to get her jacket. She had already told all her friends about getting one but they didn't believe her. When she came back with it, she'd show them. She'd have her very own Elfin Hunters' Jacket. Boy did that sound good to her ears.

On the way back, everybody stopped and stared. She was the center of attention. Very few humans ever got to wear the Hunters' Jacket, so this was special to everyone in the village. As Naida got to Zona's she noticed David leaving so she rushed inside to find Gaea. She found her upstairs, going through her clothes, looking for something to wear on her date tonight.

"I can't believe how lucky we are," Naida said, while looking at herself in the mirror. "We have gotten our dream come true."

"Yeah, isn't it great," Gaea agreed. "I can't believe I'm going on a date with David. He's so dreamy; all the girls are going to be so jealous. Even Terri wanted to get his attention. I just can't get over getting him before she had a chance."

"Well, I'm going to go show off my new jacket some more," Naida said, running out of the room.

As she came downstairs, Naida noticed Larissa and Zona in the kitchen, eating another piece of cake. Larissa called out to invite Naida to eat another piece. Even Gaea had another piece before she left to meet David. They were going to eat at the inn where everybody would see them there. Life sure was good, Gaea thought as she walked out the door.

It was just a few short hours later that Gaea came storming back in.

"I can't believe that I wasted my wish on that self-righteous, egotistical, self-centered, stuck-up macho…person," Gaea bellowed, stomping around, pulling her hair. "All he did was talk about himself the whole night. How great his hair looks, how guys are better at hunting than girls. He even told me, how lucky I was to be out on this date with him tonight. I was so stupid to waste my wish on him."

"He couldn't have been that bad," Naida said.

"Oh, yes he was and worse," Gaea replied, still fuming. "You would not believe how stuck up he is, of all the nerve."

Zona stepped in. "I take it that your wish didn't bring much happiness. Well, don't worry about it we'll talk about all that later. Now we should all get to bed. Everything will be better after you've had time to think about it."

The next morning, Naida put on her new jacket and took a stroll through Truitt but to her surprise no one paid any special attention to her. They had all seen the jacket and it was no longer special to them. She ran home, when she got to her room, she took the jacket off and threw in on the floor. It wasn't at all what she had expected. *No one even noticed it anymore.*

Naida headed downstairs and found her sisters and Zona in the kitchen. Larissa had saved her the last piece of cake. As they were finishing up Zona asked what they had learned from their experiences.

Naida started. "I think I understand the purpose of the wishes. At least, I understand that possessions can't bring you happiness. It doesn't matter how much you have it won't make you happy. The jacket didn't mean anything because I didn't earn it. When you earn something, you don't care what people think, they can't take that away from you."

"Yeah," Gaea agreed. "I learned something too. You can't depend on other people to make you happy. Happiness is something you feel because of yourself. If you are content and satisfied with yourself it will lead to happiness."

Then Larissa spoke up, "I think happiness comes from giving. I really enjoyed the cake but I liked sharing it with all of you too."

"You're all right," Zona said proudly. "Happiness doesn't come from possessions or from other people it comes from within. Being content with whom and what you are is the first step to being happy. The Ring of Happiness doesn't mean you'll never be sad or even mad but it does mean that you will not stay that way. I was beginning to wonder if you were going to make it but you came through with flying colors. This will be the biggest celebration of all."

The Ring ceremony was a festive occasion and everybody was there; Gar, the ogre, The Elf Prince, Chanook, and even Princess Sara. It was good to see Sara again, she laughed so loud when Gaea told her how she earned her Ring of Happiness. The Princess awarded the rings again. Gaea took this opportunity to tell David just what she thought about him. It was even better when Chanook asked her to sit at his table.

Naida, on the other hand, took the opportunity to give the jacket back to Chanook. It was pressed and folded nice and neat. "I would like to thank you for the chance to wear this jacket. It meant the world to me but I don't deserve it. Not yet anyway."

"I do believe, that will be temporary. If I know you, it won't be long before you earn this jacket just like you've earned your rings. When that time comes, it would be my honor to present this very jacket to you, if you would allow," said Chanook.

"The honor would be mine," Naida said, blushing.

The party lasted long into the night and the girls enjoyed every moment of it. They couldn't help but wonder what was going to happen now.

CHAPTER 12
BROOM-RIDER

It had been two weeks since the girls last ring ceremony and eight years since they had moved to Truitt. Gaea and her sisters were talking to Zona about what they hoped to do now.

"Grand-ma," Gaea began. "I think it's time for us to avenge our father's death."

"What do you mean by avenge?" Zona asked.

"You know what I mean." Gaea answered, a little irritated.

"I know that you are Ring Masters now and revenge is not something that a Ring Master can do." Zona replied.

"You mean that we can't find out what happened to our father?" Naida asked.

"No that's not what I mean at all." Zona explained. "But that's not what Gaea said you wanted. She said you wanted to avenge his death. So which is it that you want?"

"We want to find out what happened to our father and then avenge him." Larissa piped in.

"That's what I thought," Zona agreed. "Do you understand that as Ring Masters you can't just go around killing people? It's alright for you to find out what happened to Beltar but not alright to seek revenge."

"You mean we can't do anything about what happened to our father? Gaea said with her temper rising.

"It depends on what you plan to do," Zona explained. "As Ring Masters it's your duty to find the truth in matters of wrong doing. Finding the truth and seeking revenge are two different things."

"Before you get too worked up let me say that I believe you should go and search for the truth of your father's death." Zona said and then continued. "But just because Broom-rider's dragon was involved that doesn't mean Broom-rider was. There is a difference between seeking justice and seeking revenge."

"Okay," Gaea relinquished. "We will go and try to discover the truth about his death and then we'll know which way to go from there."

"Very good," Zona agreed. "Now remember things are not always as they seem. You need to find proof that Broom-rider is involved. She may not be the source of the darkness that is plaguing the land."

"You know that she is very powerful and you need to be extremely careful when dealing with her." Zona finished, fearing for their safety but knowing they had to go.

The girls decided they would leave first thing in the morning. They would travel to the Salt Flats just below Broom-rider's mountain. There they could investigate the surrounding area in hopes of discovering proof of Broom-rider's involvement. They would start with her dragon because they knew it was involved in their father's death.

When they reached the Salt Flats, Naida decided to gather some more sulfur for her supplies. The girls then trekked around the mountain to come up on the other side.

"I believe this side will be a safer way up," Gaea said. "At least they won't be watching it as much as the other."

"Yeah," Naida agreed. "There is a cave in the hills up there that will be a good place to spend the night."

"I don't like caves," Larissa said. "They are cold and dark."

"Well, we'll build a fire before it gets too cold." Gaea replied.

The girls found the cave early that evening and while Gaea and Larissa hunted for some food, Naida set up their camp in the cave. Bats had made their home in it and there were droppings all over the place.

Naida made a broom out of sage straw and swept the droppings into the fire pit. Then she poured the sulfur powder into smaller bags. It made a mess so she did it over the fire pit also. Just as she was finishing up her sisters came back with a couple of rabbits and more firewood.

"What's all this mess in the fire pit?" Larissa asked.

"It's nothing. It's just some stuff that was on the floor of the cave." Naida replied, not wanting Larissa to find out about the bats. She was already nervous about being in the cave.

"Well it looks like bird poop." Larissa said with her face wrinkled up in disgust.

Giving up on keeping it a secret, Naida said. "Well it's not; it is guano though."

"What's guano?" Larissa asked.

"It's bat droppings." Naida answered.

"BAT DROPPINGS!" Larissa exclaimed. "That's bird poop."

"No," Naida replied. "Bats are mammals not birds."

"You mean there are bats in here?" Larissa continued, "Bats that will fly into your hair and suck your blood."

"These bats don't suck blood," Naida said, rolling her eyes and silently asking for help while she stirred the ashes so the droppings wouldn't show up as much. "Let's just get a fire started and go help Gaea clean the rabbits."

As the girls were finishing up with the rabbits they heard a big explosion in the cave. When they entered they saw that the fire was blown all over the place. The wood was scattered for about 10 feet and the spit Naida had made for the rabbits was broken and over by the entrance.

"Do you think Broom-rider had anything to do with this?" Larissa asked.

"I don't think so," Gaea replied.

"Me either," Naida agreed. "I think it was that stuff I swept into the fire pit."

"What stuff was that?" Gaea asked.

"It was just some bat guano and sulfur." Naida responded, "Mixed with the ashes and embers of previous fires."

"Could that have done this?" Larissa asked, still puzzled.

"I really don't know," Naida confessed, "But I intend to find out."

"That's just one more reason I don't like caves." Larissa muttered under her breath.

The girls cleaned up again and got the fire started while Naida made another rabbit spit. Soon, they had the rabbits roasting over the fire, Naida gathered up some more of the bat guano so she could do some investigating on the combination of these ingredients later.

The next morning they started up the mountain to find Broom-rider. They reached her castle shortly after noon and decided to take the direct approach. Gaea knocked on the door and soon they heard foot steps inside the castle. Naida left her long bow hidden by the door. She still had her short bow because it was better in close quarters.

"Well, what do we have here?" Broom-rider exclaimed as she opened the door. "I must admit that your coming here is quite a surprise; a pleasure but still a surprise. It saves me from having to search for you. Come in, come in."

"You may not be so happy so see us when you find out our purpose." Gaea responded. "We've come to find out your part in all that has happened to us."

"Oh, I see," Broom-rider said smiling. "Since you're Ring Masters, you need proof of my involvement concerning the tragedies in your lives. Well, I admit to it all; the wolf in the Forbidden Woods, your father and even the snake that killed your mother. So, what are you going to do about it?"

"You're going to answer for the crimes that you've committed." Gaea said as she reached for her sword. "We're going to take you in and let the king decide your fate."

Before they reach her, she disappeared. Then they heard a disembodied voice coming from upstairs. "Did you really think it would be that easy?"

They followed the voice to an upper room that was open to the sky.

"She's here," Larissa said. "I can feel it. She may be invisible but she's as real as you or I. Gaea, you and Naida guard the door and don't let her out."

Larissa stood in the middle of the room with her knife in hand, listening absorbing the sounds of the room. Then she turned and threw the knife at a distant corner. The knife just hung there in mid-air for a moment before the girls noticed the blood and Broom-rider reappeared. The knife was stuck deep in her shoulder but before the girls could grab her; the dragon flew in between them and landed.

Broom-rider climbed up on her dragon and pulled the knife out. "You girls never cease to amaze me." She said as she threw the knife back at Larissa.

"Not so fast," Naida said as she released her arrow. It went true but the witch turned her head just in time so it merely grazed her cheek.

Gaea was running toward them just as the dragon started flapping its wings to take off. She had to duck to keep from being battered by the massive beast. Gaea was able to get one swing at its leg before it lifted out of reach.

Naida ran out to where she left the long bow, hoping to get one more shot before it was too late. It was a long shot but one she had done a thousand times before. The deadly arrow found its mark in the shoulder of the dragon. This arrow was dipped in wolf's bane and the poison quickly spread into the muscle and caused the dragon to come down.

By the time the girls reached the place where the dragon landed, Broom-rider was gone. The dragon was in agony from the poison so Gaea moved in close to end its suffering. As she looked into its eyes, she received a picture of her father draped across this dragon's back.

"Did you get that image too?" Gaea asked her sisters and then asked the dragon. "Are you saying that you brought our father here instead of killing him?"

Gaea again received the picture of her father draped across the dragon's back but this time she also saw a two-headed dragon. Gaea raised her sword and sent the dragon on its next adventure.

Dragons see death as a doorway to the next part of their life. They see it as a new beginning.

"I hope that you will find peace and joy in your next life." Gaea said as she climbed down off the dragon.

"What do you think about the visions?" Gaea asked.

"I think the second dragon was a two-headed one and that our father didn't die at Chesapeake Falls." Naida replied, still in unbelief.

"So where is he?" Larissa asked, "And what has happened to him since then?"

"I don't know," Naida said. "But we now have two leads; Broom-rider and the two-headed dragon."

"I hate the fact that she got away," Gaea said.

"Yeah, well she'll carry the scars from this encounter," Naida said smiling. "And I'd bet she won't be so happy to see us next time."

The girls went back to the castle to search for any clues as to where she may have gone or where the two-headed dragon may be. This battle was a long way from being over… but that's another story.